ALWAYS

Summer

NIKKI GODWIN

BOOK #3 OF THE DRENALINE SURF SERIES

This book is a work of fiction. Names, characters, places, and incidents either
are products of the author's imagination or are used fictitiously. Any
resemblance to actual persons, living or dead, business establishments, events,
or locales is entirely coincidental.

DEDICATION

For Gabriel Medina,
the surfer who gives me eternal inspiration, eternal hope,
and eternal summer.

CHAPTER 1

It's been sixty-three hours, but it's not like I'm counting. Alright – I'm totally counting, but it's hard not to count when Topher has ignored thirty-eight text messages and sent me directly to his voicemail seventeen times.

"Call him again," A.J. says, stretching out on my bed. "And when he sends you to voicemail, leave one telling him to answer his damn phone."

I thought maybe I'd catch a break when Alston finally went back to his own room and stopped sleeping in the spare bedroom of the guest house. Two nights of him bugging me about Topher was hard enough. Now A.J. is taking over. As much as I love them both, I just need to breathe.

"I'm going for a walk," I say, slipping on a pair of flip-flops. I grab my phone and tuck it into my back pocket. There's no way I'm leaving it here or else A.J. will call and leave Topher that voicemail all on his own.

"Does that mean I'm not invited?" A.J. asks. He props up on an elbow and gives me sad puppy eyes.

But it doesn't work. Not today. Not now. Not when I'm in absolute panic mode because my ex-boyfriend's little brother kissed me, ran, and has been avoiding me for nearly three days.

"Sorry, but this is a solo trip," I confirm. "I think I just need some air. I'll be back soon."

As soon as my flip-flops hit the sidewalk, I bolt around the house to the beach. It feels like such a cliché now that I've been living here for a few weeks, but there's a sense of freedom being near the ocean.

Right now, I want nothing more than to let the waves roll in and take all of these emotions back out to sea with them, to be forever lost among the pirate treasures and ship wreckages.

But upon reaching the shoreline, I just can't let myself be one with the ocean. Maybe it's because I'm still haunted by Topher's near-drowning. Or maybe it's the knowledge of how Shark really died and how Theo couldn't save him. Whatever it is, I just can't allow the ocean to have a piece of me.

For a moment, I understand Vin's hatred for the sea. I understand the crushing fear that it'll rip someone you love away from you. In a twisted way, I don't blame him for leaving. The responsibilities of Drenaline Surf were insane, and I know he'd rather be under the hood of a car any day. But abandoning his family like that? I refuse to feel anything for him. I just can't do it.

I back away from the shoreline and trek through the sand, my eyes focused on Colby's house in the distance. He probably doesn't know about the awkward kiss with Topher, and he won't hound me to make phone calls or send texts like my roommates have been. I could ask about his parents and what his lawyer said. I could get updates on how he's planning to fight this and strategize how we're going to save his reputation with the surf industry. Any drama is better than my own drama right now.

As I near his oversized beach mansion, Jace's black truck comes into view. Then Miles's dreadlocks. And furniture. My chest tightens and I dart back through the sand in the opposite direction. Topher and Miles were supposed to move in with Colby this weekend. Miles shouts out an order to Jace in the distance, and I panic. I'm sure the Hooligans know, and I just can't face them, even if they could force Topher into talking to me.

I rush around the closest house to hide from anyone who may be in Colby's driveway. I inhale the salty air and rest my head back against a weathered shutter. My fingers trace the peeling paint, and without a second glance around, I know exactly where I am.

This is the beach house where it all began. Linzi and I joined Alston and Reed at a beach party where I roamed the sand looking for Shark McAllister, believing he was the party boy of the group named A.J. Miles won twenty dollars from Dominic in a game of pool, and Topher popped up on the pool table moments later and introduced himself as the best surfer since Shark McAllister.

I attempt to peer through the window into a back room of the house, but the windows are hazy with remnants of sandstorms and daily beach weather lingering on the glass.

I walk around to the front porch. Tire marks streak through the sand, and summertime furniture sits by the front door. Maybe the owners go up north during the summer. I can't imagine anyone leaving Crescent Cove during this time of the year, though. Maybe it's a rental house that no one wants to rent. Or maybe it has termites. I can't fathom any other reason for this place to be abandoned.

I reposition one of the porch chairs away from the view of the street and curl up against the lime green and orange cushion. I wonder if Officer Pittman would haul me in for trespassing if I decided to stay on this porch forever. Maybe I can just sit here until the owners of the house come back and force me away. At least then I can ask them why they'd leave the most rustic beach house on the planet during the most beachy time of the year. Even more so, I'd ask them why they let the West Coast Hooligans, of all people, throw parties here.

A car door slams, and I jump up from the chair immediately. I wasn't actually serious about staying here until the owners came home, but I clearly have magical timing. I ease over to the edge of the porch and watch a shadow move around the side of the house.

The messy-haired, blue-eyed boy who emerges isn't exactly who I expected to see, but he can't avoid me now. Topher freezes in the sand and stares at me, equally as confused as I am.

"What are you doing here?" he asks.

"I could ask you the same thing, Mr. I Refuse to Answer Calls and Texts," I say, folding my arms over my chest. "I planned on staying here until the owners came home and kicked me off the porch. Apparently, they sent you to do that job, though."

He shakes his head and forces a half-smile but avoids eye contact. Then he walks toward me, up the front steps, and to the front door. He fiddles with his keys for a moment before turning to me.

"The person who owns this house isn't coming home," he says. "C'mon in."

He flips on the living room light and makes his way into the kitchen. He drops the mail on the counter and retrieves a glass from the cabinet. As he fills it with water from the filtered system on the refrigerator door, I grab the junk mail to see who lives here.

Jacob McAllister
2307 Dolphin Point
Crescent Cove, CA 56830

It amazes me how often I feel stupid for not putting the pieces together. Of course, Shark would live basically next door to Colby Taylor. Of course, the Hooligans would have access to Shark's house. How did I seriously miss the dots that connected all of this?

Topher guzzles down the glass of water. I'm not sure if he's nervous, dehydrated, or just needs a distraction, but he doesn't face me. I don't want him to catch me watching him, but I don't want to pretend to be interested in this Discover card application mailed to a dead guy either. Instead, I glance around the living room behind me. It's bare of any real décor.

Definitely a bachelor pad. Shark's photography hangs on every wall.

The clink of a glass behind me turns my attention back to Topher. The glass sits on the counter, and he rocks back and forth on the heels of his shoes.

"So, um, you want a tour of the place?" he asks.

I don't know what to make of him right now. He's obviously avoiding the real topic at hand, but I'm afraid bringing it up may send him bolting out the door.

"Sure," I say, breaking eye contact because it is definitely too awkward right now.

I keep my head down as Topher brushes past me. The scent of sunscreen and salt water is sensory overload, and I want so badly to throw my arms around him and tell him that everything is okay.

He motions his arms around the room. "Living room, Shark's photography, basic furniture," he says. "Over here, there's a ping in the wall where Theo threw a keychain that Shark gave him. I think it fell under the house or something because we never could find it later. Theo still looks for it every now and then, but he doesn't come around here much. It's too hard for him."

Not far from the living room, Topher motions around the game room, where Shark's pool table still sits center stage. As we venture into Shark's office space, which is cramped with surfboards and photography equipment, Topher doesn't make eye contact. He's completely silent once he steps into Shark's room.

"So, is this how it's going to be now?" I ask, blocking the doorway of Shark's bedroom. "You're just going to avoid me forever?"

Topher heaves a heavy sigh. He knew this was coming, but he evidently doesn't want to face it. He buries his face into his hands and groans. Then he runs his hands through his hair and falls back onto Shark's bed, once again avoiding eye contact with me and engaging more so with the ceiling.

"You know I love my brother, right?" he asks. Then he pushes up on his elbows and looks directly at me while I continue lingering in the doorway.

I nod because I can't speak. I can't believe this is how he's going to talk his way out of this. He's going to use the brother card – the same card that Miles told Vin not to use when Topher was in the hospital.

"My brother is an ass," Topher says. "Like, jerk of the year kind of ass. He pisses me off, and if I could see him right now, I'd probably hit him. But he's still my brother. He took me in when my parents kicked me out. He's the reason I graduated high school. He's the reason I have a sponsorship with Drenaline Surf. Like I said, jerk of the year, no doubt, but the jerk *is* my brother."

I wish he'd just say it. Really, I wish he'd just texted me all this instead. I think it would've been a lot easier to swallow via text. At least then I wouldn't have had to stand here and actually hear him say the words.

"He's not all bad," Topher quickly interjects into his brother-love monologue. He pushes himself up into a sitting position now. "He has a lot of really good qualities, but my point is, you were dating the wrong guy. All the things you liked about Vin weren't really Vin. They were Shark, and Vin is nothing like Shark – but I am."

What was it Vin said that day in his office at Drenaline Surf? If Shark was here, *he'd* be the one dating me. It makes sense now. I will my legs to move, but they feel like sandbags holding me to this spot, unable to budge. In a way, I'm glad because I don't want to leave an open exit for Topher to escape if this gets too weird, but at the same time, I need to be closer to him, to see the hues of blue in his eyes.

"I'm sorry for avoiding you," he says. "I'm sorry for all

the awkwardness and for being impulsive and for being a stupid guy. But I'm not sorry for kissing you," he says.

I find my footing and dare to leave the doorway. I sink onto the bed next to Topher but don't look him in the eye just yet.

Topher inhales and exhales, a bit more loudly than necessary. "I was scared," he says, finally glancing my way. "That's all I can really say. I was scared. I didn't know what you were thinking or feeling. So I ran. That's one thing I *am* good at."

"So where does that leave us?" I ask.

He forces a slight laugh. "Is there an us?"

My cheeks flush with heat, like the sunshine beating down on my skin. Even knowing that this conversation is moving in the right direction, it's still hard to actually spit out the words.

"Well, I kind of thought there was," I say. "You know, since we've finally straightened out the whole 'dating the wrong brother' issue."

A smile creeps across his face, and he narrows his eyes at me. "Are you sure you can handle me, though? I mean, that's a lot of sugar cubes and energy drinks," he reminds me. "Not to mention, I'm impulsive and do some really stupid shit sometimes, like night surfing or kissing my brother's ex-girlfriend. You just never know."

I can't help but laugh. He makes a good point, but he's forgetting who he's dealing with.

"Seriously? A.J. Gonzalez and Colby Taylor are my best friends," I say. I turn my entire body to completely face him. "And in case you forgot, I handle PR and make your completely unmarketable and currently handicapped best friend look good for the surf industry."

Topher surprisingly keeps a straight face, and for half a second, I worry that maybe I've crossed the line by stating the brutally honest facts about Miles.

"You're right," he says, cracking a smile. "You're a rock star. You can totally handle me."

"Speaking of Colby and your best friend, shouldn't you be moving in with them today?" I ask.

Topher quickly shakes his head. "Not while Miles is over there hobbling on one leg and barking out orders," he says. "I know he feels useless and wants to help, but sometimes, he just needs to get out of the way and stop trying because he only makes it worse. So I'm moving my stuff in later."

He stares at the hardwood floor, swinging his leg back and forth. "I've been staying here. I know I'm mad at Vin, but it's just too weird being at the apartment without him," he says. "It's too quiet, and I feel completely alone."

"So you stay here, in an empty house where you know the guy who owns it will never come home?" I ask.

I feel like that would be ten times worse. At least Vin can physically come back if he decides to. Topher said it himself – Shark isn't coming home.

Topher looks up from his flip-flops. The smirk on his face is adorably scary. "See, that's where you're wrong," he says in a sly tone. "I came home today, and there was a pretty girl waiting on the porch for me, so this is a much better option."

"Technically, I was waiting for Shark McAllister," I correct him.

He shrugs. "Sorry, babe, but you're stuck with the next best thing."

CHAPTER 2

"I just think it's better if you guys go in my place," Joe says from the swivel chair behind the desk.

It's weird seeing Shark's dad sitting here, grabbing the phone and sifting through e-mails in the Drenaline Surf office.

Even though I know he's hundreds of miles away working on mechanical crap for oil rigs, I keep expecting to walk in here one morning and see Vin sitting in that black chair, bitching about inventory while paying invoices and running payroll.

"Look, the store will run just fine without you here today," Joe reassures us. "I'm not the target audience for a new store. I'm old school. It's better if you see it. You'll know if it's the right fit for us. Besides, it'd be nice for you guys to represent the company. You'll be the ones handling things anyway."

I dare to glance at Jace, but he's focused on the tile flooring, thoughts running through his head like sports scores at the bottom of an ESPN channel. I want to feel sorry for him because I know how stressful this job can be, but he's the one who volunteered for it. He just needs to get out of his own head. He's a front-man for a band. If he can entertain a crowd, he can seal business deals. I need for Jace to believe in himself.

Saying that I miss Vin is absurd because I don't miss him – not in the way people would expect. But I miss his presence here at Drenaline Surf. I miss the way he had everything under control, even when he didn't. I miss that confirmation that no matter what, Drenaline Surf would be okay and it would always keep going because Vin Brooks wouldn't let it die. We're missing that spark now. Who knew Vin had a spark?

"Take Colby with you," Joe suggests. "He needs a break from all this lawsuit drama."

He doesn't have to suggest it twice. I volunteer to call him and dash out of the office as quickly as I can. I hate to leave Jace in there with the weight of responsibilities looming over him, but it's my first day back at Drenaline Surf since Vin left and this thing with Topher became official, so I'm feeling completely out of my element. Having my wingman with me for today might help me readjust to Drenaline Surf life.

Once Colby agrees to ride with us, I wait in the back parking lot with Jace.

"I haven't even started training yet," he says, shaking his head while he paces in front of me. "I mean, yeah, I can run a register and order supplies. I can manage a store because that's what I've been doing, but there's a lot I don't know."

Joe gave us a pretty compelling speech this morning. He was right about some things. It *will* take us a little while to get resituated and back on track. We *will* have to work together and just try to do the best that we can. And Joe *does* believe in us, even if we're unsure about ourselves at the moment.

Jace walks over to his driver's side, leaving me alone on the tailgate, and returns with a cigarette in his mouth. He flicks a lighter and exhales a cloud of smoke later.

"Seriously?" I ask. "You're a vocalist. You know better."

"What?" he counters. He holds up the cigarette. "This? It's a stress thing. I don't smoke on a regular basis. I'm just overwhelmed. I don't know what I'm doing. Hell, Vin knew what he was doing and *still* left."

Vin left because he's a coward and wouldn't ask for help. I bite my tongue so I don't slip up and say it out loud. It may be true, but I'm the last person who needs to say it. I have the ex-girlfriend strike against me, and dating his brother definitely wouldn't help my case.

"You're not Vin, though," I say, pushing myself off of the tailgate. Colby's truck pulls into the parking lot, and I fixate my eyes on him but continue talking to Jace. "We'll get through this. You have A.J. and Topher and me all here to help you learn how to run this place."

Jace takes a drag and exhales smoke. I leave him alone with his nicotine and make my way toward Colby's truck. The blonde surfer doesn't bother to exit his vehicle, so I open the driver's side door when I reach him.

"Don't tell me you're backing out on us," I say, hoping and praying he isn't because I don't know Jace well enough to carry on a conversation for over an hour's worth of driving.

Colby shakes his head. "Just looking at these documents my lawyer e-mailed to me," he says. "I honestly can't believe my parents are trying to sue me. I knew they'd be pissed or hurt or both, but I never thought this would end up being a money thing if they found out where I was."

I glance around the parking lot to make sure no one is nearby to hear us. "Have you gotten any closer to finding out who leaked them the info about you?" I ask.

He shakes his head again and locks his phone. "I don't even know where to start," he says. "My parents are playing it cool, like they just happened to see me on a sports channel or something, which I know isn't the truth. Someone tipped them off, and everything in me says that it was someone connected to Drenaline Surf, so I don't trust any of them, especially now with all the changes around here."

Colby will never admit it if he misses Vin, but at least with Vin, he knew what to expect. He knew what he was walking into each time he entered Drenaline Surf. It may have been like fire and gasoline, but at least it was expected.

We walk back over to Jace's truck, where I claim the passenger seat, and Colby gives Jace half-truths about what his lawyer has been telling him. Jace doesn't seem to pick up on the fact that Colby isn't very trusting of him yet, which is a good thing. We can't afford any more tension than what's already here.

"First day on the job and you get to hang out with Damage Control and her Damaged Goods," Colby says. "Do you feel like the boss yet?"

"Not quite but maybe we're getting there. Hold on," Jace says just before cranking up his truck. "Joe's calling me."

He steps outside, looks at the store for a moment, and then nods his head, although Joe can't see him from here. I wonder if there's been a change of plans. I don't really want to go to the outskirts of Sunrise Valley to see an empty lot and floor plans, but at the same time, I don't want to be in the actual store today. Topher and Emily are both working. That would lead to awkward moments with him and excited squealing from her, and none of that fits my agenda for telling people about Topher and me.

Jace opens his door and rests his arm against the doorframe. "Logan's going with us," he says. "Joe thinks it's a good idea, and Logan really doesn't have anything else to do since he's not working in the store."

Colby groans, channeling some kind of growling sea creature from the dinosaur age. I don't call him out on it because that sound defines exactly what I feel upon hearing Logan's name. Couldn't they have sent Miles and his crutches instead? At least we could just feed him to shut him up. Logan is a perfect stranger to us.

"Why all the hostility?" Jace asks, fighting a smile. "I mean, he's one of us, right? Drenaline Surf family? I mean, of all people, I expected the two of you to be more accepting of him than the rest of us."

That's what stings. I'm not sure if it's the fact that Jace is right – we are outsiders who should understand – or if it's the fact that Jace just referenced us, indirectly of course, as the outsiders of the Drenaline Surf family. Colby and I aren't from here. We're from the east coast, just like Logan. We haven't been born into this surf culture family. Even Vin, who hates the ocean and hates surfing and hates everything about the Californian hang-ten lifestyle, belongs here more than we do.

Colby clears his throat, but he's probably choking down another groan and trying to hide it.

"We don't know his story," he says. "No one knows the first thing about Logan Riley. How can we trust him with Shark's legacy when he's just a name that pops up every now and then and wins the Sunrise Valley Tournament?"

"He hasn't made an effort to know anyone here," I add, hoping to back Colby's case. "Colby made a point to meet people when he arrived. Linzi and I did the same thing last summer. Have you seen Logan around? Do you ever see him inside the store? I've seen him like three times since he got here."

Jace shrugs his shoulders and gets back into his truck. "Maybe he doesn't have a story, you know?" he asks. "Not everyone is tabloid-worthy. I'm just saying."

As much as I want to glance behind me and see the fury carved into Colby's face, I don't dare turn around. Instead, I look out the window toward Drenaline Surf. Within a few seconds, the back door of the office opens, and Joe points at Jace's truck. Logan smiles his modelesque smile before shaking hands with Joe and walking our way.

He wears a light blue polo shirt and khaki cargo shorts. His summer tan is darker than I remember, and natural highlights streak his hair. He looks so clean-cut and magazine-cover-worthy. This boy isn't tabloid fodder. Unfortunately, my sidekick in the backseat is.

Colby slides over behind Jace to let Logan sit behind me. Neither of them speak when Logan enters the vehicle. Jace looks at me, like he's waiting for me to break the ice, but when I remain frozen as well, he takes it upon himself to turn around and attempt introductions.

"I'm sure you already know who we are, but I'm Jace

Hudson, Vin's replacement," Jace says.

The words feel all too real when he speaks them. Vin's replacement. This is Drenaline Surf now. Jace is the boss. Logan is one of us. And I actually relate to Colby more than I do the rest of the 'Drenaline Surf family' right now. I definitely didn't see that coming last summer.

"This is Haley Sullivan. She's handling public relations for Drenaline Surf, and I doubt Mr. Taylor needs any sort of introduction," Jace continues. The smirk on his face is reminiscent of the icy chills and thick tension between Vin and Colby. Maybe nothing's actually changed at all.

On the hour and a half drive to the edge of Sunrise Valley, Jace talks about the music store, its lack of business, and how fortunate he was to be able to step into another job so quickly, even if he's sad that Vin left us. He asks Logan the obligatory questions about where he grew up, what his family is like, and how he likes Crescent Cove while Colby and I remain silent. I don't care if I'm an outsider. This is awkward, and I don't want to participate.

"Merge right. Drive zero point two miles. Turn right," the robotic lady announces from the GPS.

I angle myself toward the window to take in the coastline outside of Sunrise Valley. The early afternoon sunshine bursts in yellow streaks across the ocean, like watercolors floating over a canvas and trying to shift into a perfect position before drying to the surface. Jet skis zip through the waves, and bikini-clad girls tan on the beach. It's like summertime never ends here.

"Okay, I think this is the street," Jace says, pulling my attention back to the mission at hand.

We make a turn onto Coastline Boulevard, but I'm certain this isn't the same street I rode along with Alston just weeks ago before paying Topher's entry fee. There was nothing but sand and sea and a ton of cars.

"This can't be right," I say, staring at the massive building that stretches down the entire block.

It's the length of three or four football fields with a second level and floor-to-ceiling windows. A huge dome wraps around from one end of the building to the other, hiding whatever may be behind the building. And that's when I see the sign.

Future Home of Liquid Spirit Surf Shop and Wave Park

Colby exhales harshly. "You're fucking kidding me," he says. "Liquid Spirit is opening a wave park? How unethical is that?"

For the first time since we left Crescent Cove, I turn in my seat to face him. "What are wave parks exactly?" I ask.

"Artificial waves," Colby says. "They generate actual waves but in a pool or natural lagoon rather than in the ocean. It's like having full control over a swell, creating any kind of wave you want. You want tubes? You got tubes. You want double overhead? Okay. You want small waves and offshore winds for airs, you got it. It's manipulation of our sport."

Jace taps his brakes and pulls into the tiny empty lot at the end of Liquid Spirit's mega-shop. A black SUV waits for us. I recognize the guy as soon as he steps out of the vehicle. Vin was talking to him about how professional the Drenaline Surf staff was the night we arrived home from the impromptu carnival visit.

"I have some bad news," the man says, "but I have a feeling you've already seen it." He motions his arm out toward the monstrosity next to our lot.

He walks forward with his hand out. "Miller Brighton," he introduces himself. "Nice to meet you, although it's not exactly what we'd all hoped for."

"Jace Hudson," Jace says. "This is Haley Sullivan, our PR rep, and two of our surfers – Colby Taylor and Logan Riley."

Mr. Brighton loosens his tie and turns toward me. "We meet again," he says. "Although, you brought a much more somber bunch with you this time around."

He shields his eyes from the blistering sun and stares across the lot at the competition. He looks about as defeated as I feel.

"Well, I think it goes without saying, but I don't think we should build a second store here," he says. "They're moving fast to build a name for themselves, and being anywhere in this vicinity is detrimental to a smaller store."

Jace sighs. "Agreed. I guess plans for a second store are out," he says. "So much for growth and expansion."

"Don't rule it out just yet," Mr. Brighton says. "There's a place near Horn Island that may be more ideal for you guys. It's an old mechanic shop, but I think a transformation could happen. If you're up for it, we can drive back and I'll show you the place."

"Might as well," I say. I hate that we wasted our entire morning driving up here in awkward conversation for absolutely nothing. "Let's go. I already hate the sight of Liquid Spirit."

CHAPTER 3

"Liquid Spirit's mission is to bring the sport and culture of surfing to new levels and new communities," Logan says from the backseat. "Surfing is not only a sport but an art form of expression, a discovery of individuality, and an enthusiasm for adventure. We want to create an environment where those with a passionate spirit can grow and conquer their dreams."

"Generic," Colby says. "That could be a mission statement for any surf company on the planet. They want to spread surf culture, get more eyes on our sport, and cash in. More visibility means more cash flow."

If Liquid Spirit wants visibility, they're definitely going to get it. It's not like anyone can really un-see the massive store and its giant dome-covered wave pool. As much as I hate it, I know they'll thrive. Kids who've never surfed before will test the wave pool first. Parents who don't want to let their kids into the vast ocean will feel safer here. It's a monitored, controlled environment. Surfers will flock to the pool during bad weather weeks, and those who aren't against it ethically will use the control to master air reverses or how to maintain their speed in the tube. It's a breeding ground for a new generation of non-surfers to become the next big names in the sport.

Logan continues his informative speech with measurements of the wave pool – nearly 1,100 feet in length and 400 feet in width – and how convenient Liquid Spirit is for all of your surfing and beach-going needs. The wave pool alone will keep them in business. That's a never-ending need for surfboards, wax, fins, wetsuits, and surf leashes.

Jace shakes his head but never looks away from the highway. "Who do they think they are? Hurley? There's no way they can be the next big name in surf sponsorship and products," he says. "Who's footing the bill for all of this? They literally just came out of nowhere. They didn't grow and finally make it big."

I glance out the window and try to place myself back on the beach at the Sunrise Valley Tournament. What was that guy's name who wanted to sign Topher? They offered him mega-money, more than he'd ever make with Drenaline Surf.

"There's no CEO listed on their site," Logan says. "But there's a contact number if you want to call them."

Jace laughs, just barely. "No, thanks," he says, finally seeming to be back on our side. "I wonder if they knew we were looking into a lot on that street. If they've already made a move to try and sign Topher, they're obviously aware of who we are."

That's what scares me. We're trying to branch out, but we only have four surfers signed to us, and Colby's the most famous of them all – and it's not always the good kind of fame with him. What are we doing to grow Drenaline Surf? We can't afford a stadium store with a wave pool. If Liquid Spirit builds a name for itself and decides to open small branches down the coastline, Drenaline Surf could easily go under.

"If they're looking to step on the competition, a wave pool is a pretty genius way to go about it," Logan says, sending a sharp pain throughout my body.

"Genius? You think that's genius?" Colby snaps.

Oh, here it goes.

"It's a disgrace to our sport," Colby says, matter-of-factly. "Surfing is about being out there, among the waves, waiting for a perfect set to roll through. It's about the uncertainty. It's about the adrenaline rush. Will you land that air? Will you make it out of the tube? It's about how the water feels splashing against your face, how the sun feels beating against your skin. It's a moment in time. It's uncontrollable and unpredictable. That's what makes it perfect."

My fingers dig into the seat to keep me from turning around to see his face. It'd be dangerous right now to see that kind of passion burning behind his eyes. He sounds just like the guy I met at a boring corporate party in North Carolina. He sounds like the dreamer I chased across the country. He sounds like the kind of guy Shark McAllister would have taken under his wing and made into the best surfer on the west coast.

"No, I get that," Logan says. "But this is also a sport. It's for competition. There is no better training ground than a controlled wave. You can learn to master things that the ocean may not let you learn as quickly. There's less chance for injury. John John Florence may be incredible, but how often is he out with injuries?"

The ocean blurs next to us, just a long strip of greenish-blue haze pouring itself alongside the highway. I'm glad Topher stayed behind today. I'm not sure what stance he takes regarding wave pools, but with Logan name-dropping John John Florence, Topher would've probably eaten him like a Great White on a seal.

"That argument isn't even valid," Colby counters. "John John injures himself going for broke in real waves of consequence. And he's mastered it in the ocean. Pipeline is his backyard."

"Well, not everyone is fortunate enough to grow up next to the ocean with places like Pipeline in their backyards," Logan smarts back.

Colby scoffs. "We're from North Carolina," he says. "Haley and I are just as east coast as you are, if not more."

Jace reaches for the volume on the radio, says something about loving this song, and drowns out any chance Logan had to make a comeback.

"It's not as big as the lot near Sunrise Valley," Mr.

Brighton says as he searches for the correct key to this old building. "But I think it has potential to be something, with the right touch, that is."

I step back and take in the old mechanic shop. *Mallard Brothers Automotive* is painted in scratchy, faded letters over the entrance. The pastel blue paint remains only in remnants. A thick layer of dust clouds the windows, much like the back bedroom of Shark's house.

When we step inside, I can't help but wonder how long this place has been out of service. It has probably been on the market for a while, and no one bothers to keep it up. It looks as though someone came in, pushed a broom around to pretend it'd been cleaned, and then vanished without actually doing any real work. Dust particles glisten in the air around us, exposed by the sunlight trying to force its way through the dirty windows.

"Well, it needs some work," Logan says from behind me.

"You think?" Colby counters. He brushes past me and turns to face us. "This place is too small. There's no way to fit Drenaline Surf's typical inventory in here."

"He's right," I say, walking beyond Colby to look further into the building. "Even if you could fit everything, it'd just stretch back outside of the cashier's view. You're opening the store up to a lot of easy theft."

Jace sighs louder than necessary, but he knows we're right. The layout of this building won't work without overhauling the entire thing – not to mention that it needs a deep scrub because there's still car oil residue on the concrete flooring.

"Okay, so what if we don't do things like the original Drenaline Surf?" Jace asks. He walks past me, studying the layout and building plans in his head. "What if we take that wall down and move it back, so we can make a board showroom over here?"

He points to the open space out to the left that was probably once a small lobby or waiting area. I can't imagine much else other than a vending machine, a few chairs, and a bedside table fitting in there.

He walks over to the ancient front counter. "We can revamp this and leave it here," he says. "And this area to the right – we'll use it for a smaller display, maybe surfboard accessories since the showroom is the main focus. Stick the wax, leashes, whatever over here. Sort of like a 'last minute items' to go with your board."

"And what about the entire back part of the building?" Colby asks, still not seemingly sold on anything that Jace is pitching us.

Jace smiles this Vin Brooks kind of smirk that makes my heart twinge in a somewhat awkward yet nostalgic way.

"That's the best part," he says, too slyly for even my comfort level. "What if we don't turn this into a second store? What if we turn it into a custom board shop? Shark always wanted his own line of surfboards. We can do it here. We can use that entire shop for an actual board shaping shop."

Colby walks over to the counter and looks around, like he can't quite wrap his brain around everything just yet. "Okay, so the idea is borderline genius, but you're forgetting the most important part of that plan," he says. "We don't have a board shaper, and most shapers want their own business, not to work for another company. At least not long-term. They'll use you as a stepping stone until they can branch out."

Jace shakes his head. "Not if we hire someone internally who wants to do it just for Drenaline Surf," he says. "And I already know who'll do it for us."

CHAPTER 4

The atmosphere in Drenaline Surf is dismal the next morning, even though Jace's plan was well received by Joe. No one is really talking about our deepest fears, though. We all know what Liquid Spirit and its wave pool and corporate status could do to us. Joe said it himself when Jace gave him the details of our trip up the coast. This could drive us out of business. It's that simple.

Jace scribbles on the notepad in front of him, trying to create a cheat-sheet for paying invoices. I may just be the girl who talks to the media so our surfers won't slip up and say something stupid, but all that time I spent wasting away while Vin did payroll and paid bills is finally coming in handy.

"Okay, I think I've got this one," Jace says, clicking through the screen to pay the T-shirt vendor. "Invoices are easier than payroll. Hopefully I'll have the hang of all this before we have to train Alston on how to do it for the other store."

I step aside and glance out at the front counter. A.J. is in the middle of the room, making the rounds and speaking to customers. He's a natural at this management thing, even if he doesn't believe me when I tell him. Emily speaks with her hands, pointing to things on the screen, and probably overwhelming Alston with an overload of information. I should've let A.J. train him, but I feel like they'd spend more time talking than working. Topher and Miles were out of the question – they don't take the cash register nearly as seriously as Emily does.

My eyes draw away from Alston's training session when Colby walks through Drenaline Surf, speaks quickly to A.J., and then heads in my direction.

"Everything okay?" I ask, as soon as he's in earshot. "It's

not like you to show up here without a demand for your presence, and even then, there's usually some sort of scene to go along with it."

Colby laughs. "Only when Vin was here," he clarifies. "I was actually hoping I could steal you away for a bit. I need to talk to you about some things – fixing my image and stuff. You know, PR-to-surfer kind of stuff. Think you can break away for lunch?"

I glance over my shoulder at Jace, but he waves me along and says he's 'got this.' I grab my bag, let A.J. know that I'll be back, and make my way out onto The Strip with Colby. He drops his shades back over his eyes and doesn't say a word until we're secured in his truck.

"Why didn't you tell me about you and Topher?" he asks immediately. He cranks the vehicle and adjusts the air conditioner. "Of all people, I thought you'd tell *me*."

I lean my head back against the seat. "I'm just not volunteering information," I tell him. "I wasn't sure how people would react. I dated his brother, and then we had a horrible, public breakup where I was fired from my job. And then Vin left and now everything's a mess. So I really didn't think I should announce it."

"You obviously didn't think about how this would affect me," Colby says. He looks away from me in the most dramatic fashion. "Do you have any idea how stupid I looked last night when Topher and Miles were acting like this was old news and I didn't know? You have no idea how dumb I felt when Miles said, 'Dude, you're like her best friend and shit. I can't believe she didn't tell you.'"

I crack up immediately, and I'm not sure which is funnier – Colby's offended attitude or that spot-on impression of Miles. He turns onto the street and tells me that we're headed to Shipwrecked because he's craving fries after watching Miles eat half a bag of them last night.

"I thought we were tight, though," he says. "After all we've been through, the cover band and the Solomons and breaking my window…"

"Don't forget breaking that coffee table," I chime in. "Or when your parents showed up and I had to track you down on the pier. Or when you were going to quit Drenaline Surf and I was creeping in your living room waiting to give you that speech I'd prepared."

"Exactly!" he shouts at his steering wheel. "There is no one in Crescent Cove who has been through this much shit with me. You're like the one person who always has my back, even when I'm wrong. I expected better of you."

Luckily he lets me off the hook pretty easily. I guess that's the perk to being Colby Taylor's only real friend. He forgives quickly. He tells me how Topher finished moving the last of his things in last night, but he didn't unpack anything. Miles doesn't seem to be making himself at home, either.

"He's always leaving to go to Emily's house, and I overheard him telling Topher that he's trying to convince her to get an apartment with him," Colby informs me as we pull into Shipwrecked's parking lot. "He also told Topher that it's hard to live with me because I buy all that 'organic grass shit that humans aren't supposed to eat.'"

"You should've invited him today," I say. "Prove to him that you do sneak carbs sometimes, usually with me, but still. It might would've made him happy to see that you are in fact human."

Colby scoffs and shakes his head. "And ruin my reputation? Are you crazy?"

I slam the passenger side door and glance at him over the hood of his truck. "You think eating fries will ruin your reputation? Have you seen your reputation lately?" I ask.

The question remains unanswered because he knows I've made a solid point. We slide into a back booth inside the diner, away from the lunch crowd which mainly consists of construction workers. I doubt they care about anything Colby has to say, but he's surveying the room with careful eyes, just like the night we met.

I lean forward on my elbows, trying to study his face. "What is it? Do you know someone in here?" I ask.

The waitress interrupts before he can answer. We place our orders, which include extra spicy fries, and wait until she disappears to pick up where we left off.

He shakes his head. "Just making sure it's safe to talk," he says before skimming the room once more. "I didn't ask you to lunch to talk about my reputation or whatever you have with Topher," he says. "I wanted to show you something."

He picks up his phone and opens the photo gallery of screenshots. "Here. Look at this," he says, sliding his phone across the table.

I zoom in and recognize a popular surf website that I personally hate because they tend to post garbage and make surfers look badly. They have all but outright celebrated Colby's recent drama with his parents and the lawsuit. If there's a way to bring a surfer out of the ocean and into trouble, they find it and capitalize on it.

As usual, there is no one named as the author of the article, but I can see Colby's concern by the headline alone.

Drenaline Surf Newcomer Logan Riley Gets The Sh*t Deal

"They don't believe in sugarcoating, do they?" I ask, hoping Colby picks up on the sarcasm in my voice. He has his serious face on, so I'm not sure how to read him right now.

Drenaline Surf's newest surfer, Florida native Logan Riley, may end up regretting inking his contract with the California-based surf company. Although Riley has made his way to the west coast and better waves, he has been left out of the limelight in favor of even newer recruit, Topher Brooks, and the surf world's own tabloid star, Colby Taylor.

Riley's co-sponsorship with Ocean Blast Energy has done him zero favors. The high profile energy drink company has yet to release promo images with the newcomer. Colby Taylor remains at the head of their promotional material. Rumors state that Brooks and his childhood best friend, Miles Garrett (also sponsored by Drenaline Surf), have a photo shoot later this month, leaving Riley out of the loop once again.

The Floridian did, however, compete in and go on to win the recent Sunrise Valley Tournament. The scandal? He wasn't meant to surf in the event in the first place. Drenaline Surf's Colby Taylor and Miles Garrett were slotted to compete, and Topher Brooks surfed on his own name prior to his sponsorship. Riley was a last-minute replacement as Garrett broke his leg in a free surf before the competition.

"Send those shots to me," I say, sliding the phone back to Colby. "I'll let Jace know."

"You think it's weird? Because I do," he says. He scans the room again. "I feel like someone's trying to bring us all down. I know, I know – I'm paranoid. I know I've been paranoid for years, and old habits die hard, but I just...I don't know. I feel it. My parents show up. Vin leaves. Now this?"

I take a deep breath and watch my phone light up as Colby's texts roll in, sending the evidence to my phone. I want to believe this is all coincidence. When it rains, it pours – or something to that effect. The universe is testing us. We're being pushed to make sure we can survive any storm. Drenaline Surf is strong, and we have to prove it. It's not a conspiracy.

"Haley, admit it," Colby says. "You think I'm right."

I exhale. "I can't," I say. "If I admit it and put it in the universe, then it becomes real, and that's when things get really scary."

We're silent as the waitress brings our lunch to the table. Colby thanks her and fakes a smile. Then he looks at me. "I don't know about you, but this already feels real, and I'm already scared."

When Colby drops me back off at Drenaline Surf an hour later, I stand outside on The Strip and try to steady my breathing. I don't want anyone to pick up on my concern. I don't want A.J. or Emily or Alston or anyone else to see the worry written on my face.

I push through the door and manage to slip by with a half-wave before closing the office door behind me. Jace looks up from the computer screen.

"What's wrong?" he asks immediately.

So much for a brave face.

"You need to see this," I say, completely defeated. I hand over my phone and watch the dread sink into Jace's skin as his eyes trace the words.

He looks tired when he turns toward me. "Can we just keep this between us for now?" he asks. "I'd rather not make a big deal out of it. Maybe it'll blow over."

I nod and keep my mouth shut about Colby's knowledge. I'm not really sure how Jace feels about my east coast friend. If he's anything like Vin, Colby probably isn't his favorite person, and it's a fire I'd rather not play with.

"Do me a favor, though," Jace says. "Keep your eyes open for any local competitions, even if they're small. When you find one that seems good, stick Logan in it. Just Logan. You know, to be on the safe side."

I continue to nod, unsure of what I should say. Is this how it'll always be with us? Will I always feel like he's an awkward stranger, even though I've been around him for a little while now? Will I always secretly wish it was Vin sitting in this office, even though fighting with him would've been inevitable?

A knock on the office door jerks me back to the issue at hand. Joe steps inside, all smiles, but his happiness quickly fades upon seeing us.

"Did something happen?" he asks, eyeing Jace more so than me.

Jace quickly shakes his head and laughs it off. "Nah, just a long day with a lot of learning," he says. "I'm just trying to take it all in. But we're good."

Joe smiles. "You'll catch on sooner than later, I promise. I know you," he says. "I bring good news, so maybe that'll help. I spoke with Rob, and he's all in for this board shop. He's looking to retire soon and get out of the business, and until now, he's had no one to pass his knowledge down to."

The words float around me like the dust particles from the new shop – small and scattered but sparkling with hope and light, like tiny stars bouncing around in a dark galaxy, trying to find their ways to each other to form a supernova and light up the universe.

Rob Hodges. He's the guy whose board shaping convention we never made it to that day when Emily convinced Miles to paint a lizard on his face. I instantly smile when I remember her squealing about being their own little garden. I'm really glad we took the wrong exit. That day was worth the epic Brooks brothers' showdown that happened hours later.

"I want you to bring Theo over to my house," Joe tells Jace. "I know he avoids me, and you can't deny it for him. I understand his guilt, but he's always been part of my family. I want this for him. Jake would've wanted this for him. This is my chance to give him the dream that my son didn't get to."

And that alone is all the hope I need. Theo will be our supernova.

CHAPTER 5

"You can't do this to me," Miles says with a groan. He leans against Colby's kitchen counter, only one crutch under his arm. "I'll starve to death while you're gone."

Topher gives him a dramatic eye roll but doesn't bother with a comeback. It's hard to believe that Miles has actually calmed down in the last hour since I broke the news to him that I was going with Topher this weekend in his place. It makes sense for Ocean Blast Energy not to want him for the photo shoot. A surfer on crutches isn't exactly what you want in a magazine ad. But it does ruin all of Miles's plans for the next two days.

I hesitate before speaking, but I refuse to walk on eggshells around Miles Garrett. "You can't buy groceries?" I ask.

He shakes his head. "I never go grocery shopping. My mom just always had food in the fridge. When I go to Emily's, she's stocked up for me. If Topher leaves me here for the weekend, I'll shrivel up and die," he says, in the most serious fashion.

I bite down on my lip to avoid laughing. I bet Miles is the kind of guy who lies in bed moaning and whining when he has a cold. Mr. Tough Guy isn't really all that tough.

"Have you seen the shit Colby buys?" Miles asks me. He nods toward the cabinets. "Even his damn pasta noodles are organic. Who makes fucking organic noodles? That's supposed to be carbs and the good stuff. He's like a damn cow out in a field with his organic lettuce and shit. I'm not even kidding."

As if being summoned, Colby steps in through the back patio door. He glances at us but doesn't say anything before heading back to the shower. I have to give him credit. He probably wants this pro surfer gig more than anyone else in Crescent Cove or Horn Island. That boy trains more than Miles or Topher even think of training.

"I'm taking you to Emily's," Topher says, grabbing his keys off the counter. Then he glances at me. "I'll pick you up tonight. Six, right?"

I nod and he shoots me a smile before rushing out of the house with Miles. Hopefully Emily has enough food stocked for this weekend. I have a feeling Miles won't bother hanging out around his new home.

I settle in on the couch in the living room. Colby joins me moments later, hair freshly washed and messy. He glances around before speaking. "Looks like the new roomies didn't want to stick around," he observes. "I'm guessing it'll be a quiet weekend."

"Miles is going to Emily's," I tell him.

He sits in the opposite corner of the couch and nods. "I figured he would. He's always bitching to Topher about how I don't have food here. He thinks I can't hear him, but he's loud," he says. Then he shrugs. "So you sure about this whole weekend away with the boyfriend thing?"

Oh God. Are you serious? Who does he think he is? Alston and A.J.? Colby's the one person who hasn't been curious my personal choices thus far. I don't need him joining my roommates in their conversations about me.

"It's a business trip," I say, even though I know he won't buy it. "He has a photo shoot. I'm taking Miles's room. It's not a honeymoon."

"Well, I'd hope not...considering," he says without elaborating.

Now the hesitation sets in, though. Maybe Colby Taylor isn't the best person to go to for guidance or advice. Hell, he wasn't the kind of person I needed to be chasing across the country. Even when his heart is in the right place, his head usually isn't. But I can't help feeling that maybe he has a point. Maybe this is all too soon, too sudden. Vin's only been gone for about two weeks, and this relationship is super new. Even if we take it slow, people will talk, and more gossip is the last thing Drenaline Surf needs.

"Look, nothing's going to happen," I say. "I can't afford for anything to happen or to even look like it's happening. Drenaline Surf's reputation depends on me right now. I'm not going to be the one to drag us down."

Colby shakes his head. "I'm not worried about you," he says. "It's just…sometimes, in this industry, people lose focus. We're surfers. We're on the beach all day, hanging out, getting wrapped up in it all. Just keep a tight grip on the reins with Topher. I could see the whirlwind catching up to him."

I don't like admitting that he's right, but Topher's career path is going to be vastly different from Colby's.

And I'm not sure if I can manage it.

CHAPTER 6

After watching Topher play professional surfer all afternoon with Ocean Blast Energy, I rethink Colby's worries that Topher may lose his sense of self in this business. Sure, surfing is their passion and hobby, but it's still a business that I think Topher will be able to navigate easily. He's got the personality for it, much like his brother, even if he would flip out if he heard me say that.

"We're going out tonight," he says from across the kitchen counter at the condo we're staying in. "There's this really awesome beach party celebration thing going on, and we're going."

"Were you invited?" I ask from the barstool.

He shakes his head. "It's not like a *party* party," he explains. "It's almost like a festival or something. They have it every summer here, and I think you'll like it. Besides, Ocean Blast is paying for us to stay here another night so we might as well make the most of it. It starts in like an hour so get ready."

A smile sweeps his face, and his eyes glisten like moonlight against the waves. There's no way I can say no, even if I wanted to – but I don't want to. I change into a tank top and shorts, much less professional than what I wore to our meeting with Ocean Blast Energy earlier today, and grab the smaller purse that I borrowed from Emily. Topher still looks like a surfer – board shorts and a Drenaline Surf T-shirt. He bounces with excitement all the way to his vehicle.

The drive to the boardwalk is much longer than necessary, but being on the edge of Sunrise Valley, it's to be expected. Topher hasn't mentioned Liquid Spirit, although I know he knows, and I don't dare bring them up right now. But seeing the size of Sunrise Valley, how the entire city is immersed in surf culture, I'm scared. Crescent Cove may be a gorgeous little beach town, but it's still little. It's a retirement area. Why bother with our tiny town when you have all it has to offer and more just an hour and a half north?

"Looks like we may have to walk," Topher says, stretching his neck in an attempt to see around the cars ahead of us. "I'm going to pull into that parking garage. At least it's close to the boardwalk."

It takes another twenty minutes, though, to even get into the parking garage and find the elevator back to the ground level. This city is crawling with vacationers, locals, and party-goers who are just here for the drinks and bonfires.

Topher slips his hand into mine and keeps me close to him as we fight our way through the crosswalk and over to the beach. A hazy sunset falls behind the ocean, pinks and purples dancing together across the sky like melted cotton candy. The waves glow with the colors of the sky, like a computerized ocean in a fantasy movie rather than reality.

"What are they celebrating here?" I ask, hoping Topher can hear me over the crowd of people. "There are like a million people here."

He laughs. "Everyone from like three towns over comes out for this," he says. "It's a pretty huge deal."

A banner stretches across the boardwalk that reads *Sunrise Valley Seahorse Memorial Celebration* in big turquoise letters. Did Topher really bring me to a celebration for dead seahorses? Solomon has been my guiding light. The last thing I need right now is his death. How is this even a good idea?

"Whoa," I say, jerking his arm back and stepping out of the line of the crowd. "Seahorse Memorial? I don't want to celebrate the lives of dead seahorses. How is that something I'd actually like?"

Topher shakes his head quickly, but his face is concerned. "It's not like that. I read about it online," he replies. He motions toward the boardwalk. "It's like this huge celebration for seahorses…but you know, in a good way?"

Part of me wonders if Topher even read about this thing or if he just heard something about a seahorse celebration on the beach and thought it was a good idea.

"Okay, if you're sure," I say, even though I'm not sold on this at all.

"Look, I wasn't supposed to tell you, but Colby told me to bring you here. Apparently, he's been before, and he said I had to bring you because it's perfect – his words," Topher says with pleading eyes.

I can't deny him any longer. I interlock my fingers with his and continue forth toward the pier that harbors the boardwalk and all of the festivities of the night. Topher hands over the entrance fee and gets our plastic bracelets for access to the pier. The girl asks if this is our first time coming to the celebration. She directs us toward a group of people down on the sand upon hearing it is.

We find a seat on a wooden log carved with tribal designs. A bonfire blazes before us, but it's small and controlled, unlike some of the crazy ones I've seen at the Hooligans' beach parties. An older lady who looks as though she could be Kale's grandmother sits at the head of the fire. A woven blanket with brilliant colors rests over her shoulders, blocking her from the breeze that gusts in from the ocean. I sort of feel like I'm in a Twilight film waiting for tribe secrets to be revealed.

People crowd in around us, chattering about last summer's celebration and how they love coming out here. The leather-skinned lady raises her hands upward, and the audience falls silent, as if they know what's about to happen.

"Tonight, there will be a full moon," she begins, waving her arms open wide toward the sky. Yep. We're definitely in werewolf territory. "And tonight, that full moon will change the tides. The ocean will not be the same."

She speaks with a serious yet dramatic tone, like she's going to lunge forward toward the fire and scream bloody murder just to scare us at any given moment. But she remains fairly still. I, on the other hand, feel incredibly antsy sitting here with strangers listening to a woman blab about the moon.

"It was long ago when they reigned supreme," she says, her face narrowing toward the fire. "It was during a time when mermaids were not afraid to swim near the surface. The ocean was a place of pure magnificence, no dangers but those of the waves in a storm. It was glorious with colors – beautiful, angelic fishes…so vibrant, so large. And seahorses, studded with jewels, that would someday be harnessed for greed. And the songs of the mermaids. All blended into a mirage of colors and life and beauty."

She speaks with conviction, like she truly believes that mermaids are frolicking in the depths of the oceans, unwilling to surface for fear that humans may see them. In a way, I want to believe it as well, just to know that Shark isn't alone out there, that maybe someone is singing his soul into a realm of peace.

"The seahorses embodied what sea royalty should be," she continues, punching her fist into the air. "They were regal, kings of the sea. Friends of the mermaids and family to the majestic fishes. As large as a human, as gentle as an elephant, more beautiful than a sunset."

I try to envision Solomon as one of these real life sea kings – cerulean blue with sapphires and diamonds sparkling over his fins and around his eyes, human-sized and royal. He'd be beautiful, at the very least.

She continues talking about the angel fishes and how brightly colored they were, how they floated among the waters like gentle giants, catching rays of sun and bouncing them around to form rainbow prisms among themselves in the water.

"But the ships could not appreciate their beauty. Evil men, hungry with greed, hunted them, preyed on them like monsters," she says, her voice intensifying and echoing around us.

I wish I could tune her out. I don't want to hear about their tragic ends. I want to imagine an ocean where seahorses still rule the ocean kingdoms. But she tells of spears piercing through them, angelic fishes floating dead at the surface, and mermaids dying and being captured during rescue missions.

"This is where piracy began," she explains. "The jewels within their skins were the original treasures of the sea. The pirates sailed the waters, in search of the next jewel, the next color to add to their chests. Slowly and surely, they took what they wanted, destroying the life below the waters."

And that's when it happened – the moon exploded. I shift my eyes at Topher to make sure I'm hearing this lady correctly. But she lifts her arms widely toward the sky and says it again.

"Her anger was becoming of her," she lady says, with a hint of a smirk. "She controlled the tides, and she decided to take back what belonged to her."

The legend states that on that fateful night, when the moon was full, a terrible storm swept over the oceans, sinking ships and their chests of treasures. The mermaids scattered, retreating to the ocean bottoms for protection, and in the wake of the madness, hid the jewels of their beloved seahorses so deeply that no pirate would ever find them.

And of course, the moon exploded. But it didn't just explode into dust. The moon erupted into thousands of bean-shaped rocks, "moon beans" as they were called.

"When they hit the water, the angel fishes and seahorses shrunk to the size of the beans, making them hard to find in the vast scheme of things," she says, holding up a bean-shaped rock that looks as though it could be made from a piece of the moon. "And every small creature – the whales and dolphins and sharks – were suddenly enlarged. No longer were they the tiny fishes that swam in the distance. They were now the protectors of the seas, a royalty of a more vicious kind, a role they still play to this day."

Oh, what I'd give to time travel back to those days, to see life-sized seahorses adorned with jewels and hear the mermaids sing their enchanted songs. Shark McAllister would've taken photos of giant yellow angel fishes rather than Great Whites. I wonder what kind of nickname he would've had instead. Shark would be out of the question.

"But tonight, on the full moon, we celebrate the true kings of the sea," the lady announces. "We celebrate them with colors and jewels and beauty. For tonight, the giant killers in the ocean shall shrink back to their true sizes, spend the night in a state of rest, and prepare for another year of protecting the true royalty. For tonight, the seahorses shall return to their glorified state, in true size, to swim in the oceans that belong to them."

Cheers erupt around us. I wonder if these people have heard this story before or if they are first timers like Topher and me. Our storyteller encourages everyone to join in the festivities, to enjoy the night like we're part of the sea, celebrating our leaders in their night of freedom. Topher grabs my hand and leads me back up the pier. We flash them our bracelets and keep going. Booths of masquerade masks and face painting artists line the entrance of the pier.

"I think we're a little underdressed," I say, glancing around. I make my way toward a table of masks to see the selection. The face paintings are much more elaborate and pretty, but I want something to take home with me after tonight.

"Should I assume you're going with blue?" Topher asks. He smiles when I glance up at him. "I mean, it's your seahorse color, right?"

That it is. I choose a half-mask that wraps itself in a crescent-shaped seahorse. The seahorse itself is a mix of turquoise and cerulean blue with an array of blue rhinestones adorning it. Topher chooses a similar Phantom of the Opera style mask with red hues. He's fine in board shorts and his Drenaline Surf merch, but we stop at another vendor to let me grab a blue gypsy-style wraparound skirt to tie over my cut off shorts.

Although the reason for celebration is enchanting and magical, it's still quite the commercial event for Sunrise Valley. Booths line the pier just like The Strip back in the cove. There are carnival games where you can win stuffed sea creatures, funnel cakes that I'm sure A.J. would love, and multiple artists much like Emily selling homemade items that fit tonight's theme. She and Miles should've come with us. Maybe next year she can.

Further down the boardwalk, a restaurant is buzzing with customers and live entertainment. Metal tables sit outside like a coffee shop, and strings of twinkle lights sparkle against the backdrop of a California night. They remind me of fireflies who never lose their light, who just sparkle in place until it's time for a long sleep. The sounds of bongo drums and ukuleles float across the night air, and Topher pulls me toward him.

"Dance with me," he says, as if we've never had this moment before.

But tonight, for Solomon and the seahorses, I don't even hesitate. I let myself fall into Topher's arms, and we dance like we've never had this moment before.

CHAPTER 7

The whirlwind of seahorse celebrations and a long, lazy day on the beach both slip away the moment we step inside Colby's house. Part of me wishes I'd gone home first, just to hang on to the lingering glow of the twinkle lights that I can still see in Topher's eyes when he smiles. Why couldn't this weekend last forever? Or, you know, at least a week? I need a longer Drenaline Surf vacation.

"Get in here and watch this shit," Miles says, reaching across Colby's couch for the remote. He rewinds the DVR and pauses it on Colby's parents.

It's definitely back to reality. No more seashores stories or masquerade masks. No more ukuleles and browsing expensive vendor booths for the perfect souvenir for Emily, the only one who'd truly appreciate it. We're back in Crescent Cove with Colby's parents on TV and Miles on crutches.

We settle in between the two blonde surfers, Topher next to Miles and myself next to Colby. Then Miles hits play.

"I'm joined today by Linda and Paul Burks, the parents of surf star Colby Taylor," a girl's voice says, even though the camera remains on the parental units.

Colby's mom sits stoically, dressed in a business suit and a pearl necklace. His father looks less professional, simply wearing a polo shirt and khakis. I expected him to look the part of a lawyer or businessman. Maybe he's hoping the downtrodden father act will gain him sympathy.

The camera zooms out, capturing their interviewer on screen. I recognize her. The blonde in the high heels.

"Oh my God. Isn't she the one who had the interview with you for SurfTube? Bridget something?" I ask, turning toward Colby.

"Yeah, four inch heels in the sand? That's her. Bridget

Parker," he confirms. "What a bitch."

Bridget tucks her hair behind her ear and angles herself toward the camera, as if she's trying to get her best side while conducting the interview.

"It's been a rough few weeks for you guys, understandably, and I appreciate your taking the time to sit down with us and help surf fans and our community understand exactly what's going on," she says, giving them a sympathetic smile.

Mrs. Burks is the first to speak. "Thank you for giving us an opportunity to explain things," she says. "It's been such an emotional time for us, and I never dreamed we'd be in this situation. Although we're relieved that our son is alive and well, we're heartbroken over how this has played out."

The creases under her eyes crush together as she squeezes her eyes closed, as if she's in massive pain and trying to brave her way through it.

"Bullshit," Colby mutters.

Bridget clears her throat. "If you don't mind, we'll begin with a few questions," she says, waiting for a nod before moving forward. "Is it true that you don't support your son's career choice?"

"Oh, no, not at all," Mr. Burks says. "He's done well for himself, as anyone can see. It may not have been the path we'd have chosen for him because it's not something you can fully depend on, but he's clearly talented and was able to make a name for himself."

His parents continue a well-rehearsed speech about how they've begged and pleaded with their son to let them be involved in his life, but he's consistently shut them out.

"We offered to move our lives to California," his mom says, fighting back a sob. "I would leave my life behind to be part of his if only he'd let me. We spent our life savings trying to find him, and this is how we're repaid just for loving our son."

Colby jumps up from him couch and paces across the room for a moment before walking over to the kitchen counter. He keeps his back toward us. Miles pauses the DVR.

We spend about thirty seconds in the eeriest silence before Colby spins around. "*I* offered to move them out here, pay for it all," he says. "I told them I'd made a name for myself, that I had a career. I'm *somebody* here, even if no one believes that. *I* offered to fix this, to foot the bill and buy them a condo on the beach. That was all *me* – not them."

Miles and Topher exchange a subtle glance, but it's enough to make my paranoia twinge just a bit. To anyone else, it would've been nothing. But I know the Hooligan bond runs deep – deeper than the Drenaline Surf brotherhood. I'm not sure of a percentage, but there's a part of them that doesn't believe him.

"Turn that off," Colby says, pointing toward his flat screen. "I can't deal with watching it again."

Miles grabs the remote and powers the TV off. The three of us remain on the couch, awkwardly trying to figure out what to say, until Miles finally looks over at Topher.

"I'm starving. You wanna drive me somewhere to get some real food?" he asks.

I don't look back at Colby because I'm certain he's shaking his head in some kind of disgusted fashion because Miles does nothing but complain. Maybe I should convince Emily to get an apartment with Miles, for everyone's sake.

After moving my luggage from his truck to Colby's living room, Topher gives me a quick kiss and runs back to his truck to leave with his best friend. I don't mind, though. I know the Hooligans aren't fully sold on all this Colby Taylor drama.

"Are you okay?" I ask, leaning on the granite countertop bar in Colby's kitchen.

He stares at his refrigerator at the picture of him with

Shark on the boat. I remember him telling me about that day, how Topher and Reed were with them. I wonder if Topher feels torn in the mix of all of this. His loyalty lies with the Hooligans, with Horn Island and all of its grit, but he trusted Shark, and Shark believed in Colby.

"I just keep letting him down," Colby says more to the photograph than to me. "I keep telling myself that if he were here, he'd have my back. He'd be on my side. But then shit like that happens and part of me wonders if anyone really believes in me anymore. Miles thinks I'm the scandal of the year, and if Topher didn't think it before, he does now."

"You're perceptive," I say, forcing myself off of the counter. I walk across the kitchen to see if I can read his face. "But you always assume everyone thinks the worst of you."

"Because they do," he says. His eyes focus on the image ahead of him, still refusing to look at me. "He told me we could handle this, that we could get through anything. He used to say that if my secrets were ever out, we'd handle it. He'd make sure it didn't ruin me. And then he died and left me here to figure it all out on my own."

I grab his shoulder and jerk him back, forcing him to pull away from the blonde wild child in the photo and see the girl in his kitchen.

"Hey!" I half-shout. "You are *not* alone in this. What am I? Vapor? Were you not the one who said all those lines about the cover band and the Solomons and breaking your window? Remember me? The girl who chased you across America thanks to your chewed gum? Is that not devotion enough for you?"

He doesn't want to crack a smile, but he can't fight it. "I know I have you. You're the only friend I have here," he reassures me. "I just miss Shark, especially when things go down like this. He always had a plan, something in mind for how to talk our way out of things. He always told me that if this came back to bite me, we'd make it through."

"And we will," I say. "If Shark said we'll make it through, we'll make it through."

The excited atmosphere in Joe's living room is vastly different from the stark realities of Colby's living room earlier today. We haven't even stepped inside yet, but happiness is looming on the other side of that screen door.

"You okay?" A.J. asks, waiting a moment before he lets everyone know we've arrived.

I nod. "Just dwelling on all this stuff with Colby's parents," I tell him. I glance around to make sure no one is lurking around outside for a smoke break or some fresh air. "Announcing this second store is just opening the door for them to raise their money bar even higher."

A.J. releases the door handle and steps back toward me. We walk back down the wooden steps and onto the sand in Joe's driveway. A.J. lights a cigarette for good measure.

"Have they sent any more papers?" he asks, keeping his voice low.

I shake my head. "Not yet anyway," I say. "But it's only a matter of time before there are court dates and negotiations. I keep telling Colby not to pay them off because it'll be a never-ending cycle. They'll always come back wanting something else from him."

"Then we'll fight it," A.J. says. He blows a stream of smoke into the air, exhaling it like he's breathing out all of his worries. "They can't drag this on forever. They have to pay the lawyer, you know? And Strick's dad hooked Taylor up with the best lawyer around. He'll be okay."

After A.J. drops the cigarette butt and stomps it out with the toe of his shoe, we venture back onto Joe's porch. I take a deep breath and remind myself to smile. I don't want Joe knowing about the SurfTube interview or my constant fear that the Burks family may lower the hammer on us any second. Shark's dad deserves so much more than that, especially right now. He's continuing his son's dream. He's building a legacy. I refuse to rain on that.

A.J. pushes the door open and makes his way over to Reed and Alston. It makes me smile to see Reed here. Even though he doesn't work for Drenaline Surf, he's always included, a real part of the Drenaline Surf family. I begin walking toward my roommates, following A.J.'s path, but Topher waves me over to him instead. He sits with Miles and Emily.

Emily slides over to make enough room for me between her and my boyfriend. Topher slips an arm around me and hugs me closer to him.

"Something big is about to happen," he informs me. A smile stretches across his face, a little too enthusiastic for me. "I'm so excited."

I lean into him so no one else will hear me. "You are aware that I know about the board shop, right? I'm PR. I'm in the loop," I whisper.

He scrunches his nose and shakes his head. "You're not in this loop."

I know he's just playfully flirting, and whatever this big secret is must be over the top because he's bouncing like he does when he has too much Ocean Blast Energy to drink. But that last comment hits a nerve. How many loops am I not in around here? And will I ever be in them? Is it possible for someone like Colby, Logan, or me to actually fit in here like we truly belong?

Before I can glimpse around to see if Colby or Logan showed up tonight, Joe takes center stage in the living room and halts all interaction. He thanks everyone for coming over on short notice and says that he has a very special announcement to make.

After explaining Shark's dream of having his own board shop someday under the Drenaline Surf logo, he invites Rob Hodges across the room to join him. It's already been decided and discussed with Theo, but they formally make a show of offering him the paid apprenticeship with Rob to become Drenaline Surf's official board shaper.

I hate that all eyes are focused on Theo at this moment. Luckily that shaggy brown hair of his hangs over his face. He looks more like a stoner teen than a twenty-something soon-to-be board shaper. He simply nods in acceptance before Rob continues with a speech of his own.

"Years ago, when I left the world of professional surfing so I could shape boards for the new generation, I had no idea what kind of mark I'd leave on the shaping world," Rob says. He wears a tan button-up shirt with a palm tree print. He's definitely from that hippie era of surfers, just like Joe.

"My biggest fear was not having someone to pass my knowledge on to," he continues, motioning a hand toward Theo. "It's not every day that you're given an incredible career in this industry. I've done my time as a pro surfer. I've served as a board shaper. And now, I get to pass my skills on to a very deserving young man to carry on two different legacies."

I almost wish Rob hadn't brought up the legacies. Yes, this was Shark's dream, but our Hooligan doesn't need any more pressure on him. Jace said it took a lot of conversation and persuasion to even get Theo to accept the position. Even now, he doesn't feel worthy.

Topher squirms next to me, biting down on his lip to keep from exploding with sugar cube happiness. He doesn't even look at Miles, which makes me wonder just how crazy this other piece of news may be. Obviously we're about to find out.

Joe swaps glances with Rob before speaking. "Because our new location is going to need a major overhaul and renovation, Rob has been kind enough to donate the funds to establish our new business and get it up and going," Joe announces. "And due to his generous contribution, we felt it was only right to take the budget allotted for renovation and invest in something else that may help grow our brand."

He can't finish his train of thought, though, because Joe cracks up. "Topher, I'll let you have the honors," he says, waving the blue-eyed surfer forward.

Topher jumps up and stakes his spot in the center of the room. Rob hands him an envelope, which Topher accepts all too happily.

"In this envelope," he says, holding it up for everyone to see, "I have a few pieces of paper that desperately need signatures. On these papers are terms and agreements for a sponsorship with none other than Drenaline Surf, and I'm so freaking happy to offer it to my favorite Hawaiian Hooligan, Mr. Kale Nakoa!"

Miles shouts a 'hell yes' and I'm thankful it wasn't a 'fuck yes' in this environment. Emily squeaks with excitement, and the bromantic hugs among the Hooligans go on for minutes before Kale thanks Joe and Rob for this opportunity before immediately signing his contract for a career in surfing.

I feel like I'm going through the motions with congratulations and smiles. But deep down, I'm suffocating. Another surfer on our roster? That's another career I have to manage, another Hooligan who may not take my career or image advice, another surfer to enter in competitions, and one more thing that makes Drenaline Surf look like a clique who only sponsors people within our surf family.

CHAPTER 8

"Well, that didn't take long," A.J. says, sliding his phone across the counter to me. He bites into a piece of toast and crunches it while waiting for my reaction.

The website logo makes me cringe. It's the same site that posted the article about Logan a week ago. Why are they out for Drenaline Surf's blood?

Alston leans into my arm, digging his chin into my shoulder so he can read along with me. Aside from breathing, neither of us makes a sound while I scroll down the screen of A.J.'s phone to take in the slander that's being tossed at us today.

Just mere weeks after Vin Brooks' sudden departure from Drenaline Surf, the crew has dropped a pretty penny on yet another sponsorship – this time, Hawaiian native but current Horn Island resident, Kale Nakoa.

Following our recent article about Logan Riley and his possible mistake in signing with Drenaline Surf, we'd hoped to make a statement and show Drenaline Surf what they look like to the outside world. Maybe the article went unread. One can assume as much seeing as they've yet again proven they are more of a cult than a surf company with the surf industry's best interests at heart.

Did Drenaline Surf call for surfers to send in video clips? Did they announce that they were looking to build their platform? We've seen none of the sort. (However, if you have links, by all means, post them in the comment section below!)

Are we the only ones who find it strange that Vin Brooks was the only person who tried to recruit and bring in fresh blood by sponsoring a talented east coast surfer? He gave Logan Riley a better opportunity and was suddenly banished from all things Drenaline Surf. No one has even seen him around town since his departure from the company. It leads us to believe that his exit may not have been as mutual as Drenaline Surf is portraying it to have been.

"Damn," Alston says, pushing himself off of me. "That's harsh. Have you guys issued any kind of press statement on Vin leaving?"

I shake my head, but I have a feeling that's what I'll be doing today. I reach across the counter and grab the least burnt piece of toast.

"Breakfast to go," I say. "I've gotta get to Drenaline and see if this has made its way around yet. Jace is new to this, and he won't be prepared. We have to issue some kind of statement, even if he wants to keep it quiet. This isn't going away."

A.J. and Alston say they'll see me at work before I head back over to the guest house to grab my bag. The drive to the store is super short, but it feels like an eternity today. I'm in damage control mood, and I'm determined to actually *do* my job today.

The Strip is quiet for the early morning hours. A few vendors are already setting up for the day's tourist crowd. One says 'good morning' as I rush by in my frantic hurry. It's anything but a good morning for Drenaline Surf. I normally enter through the back door, but I'm thrown completely out of sorts today. I fiddle with my keys and unlock the main entrance, quickly locking it again behind me.

Voices drift from the back office, and then the telephone rings. Jace answers with a, 'Drenaline Surf, Jace speaking,' that sounds stressed. Logan peeks his head out of the back office and advances in my direction.

"Morning," he says, shoving his hands into the pockets of his cargo pants. "I came up here early to talk to Jace about some things that were being said about me online."

I nod. "How you're going to regret inking your deal with Drenaline Surf?" I ask. I'm way ahead of this guy.

"You already know?" he asks, a bit surprised.

I can't fight a smile. "It's my job to know, Logan," I remind him. "I have to be in the middle of it all. I'm damage control, which I think Jace needs this morning."

We walk back to the office where Jace is telling someone on the other line that we don't have a comment at this time. He slams the phone down immediately after.

He glances up at us, defeat written all over his face. "Every local news outlet is calling here," he says. "The TV channels. The newspapers. The gossip columns. How the hell did Vin handle all of this?"

"Because he was good at his job," I say. I throw my hand over my mouth. I cannot believe I just said that out loud. "He was good with people," I correct myself. "He knew how to tell them what they wanted to hear. He could spin a story any way he wanted."

"Master manipulator," Logan says, his tone sly and borderline offensive.

"No. Vin wasn't like that," I say. I have no idea why I'm defending him. He manipulated all of us when he secretly planned his departure and abandoned us. "He wasn't like that in the business world, anyway."

Jace runs his hands through his hair and leans back in the office chair, almost like he's still not really comfortable in this new job position. "I can't spin this," he says.

I sit down on the corner of the desk. "But I can," I assure him. "I've seen Vin do this too many times with Colby. I can spin a story. Believe it or not, Vin taught me well. That's why I'm your damage control girl."

For the next hour, Jace and I pen the perfect press statement while Logan helps Topher and Emily on the front registers. We're booming with business this morning, which goes to show that all publicity really is good publicity. It's almost like people are lingering with their shopping or 'forgetting items' just to come back inside in case something happens.

"It won't stop the phone calls," Jace says, sitting in front of the Drenaline Surf website.

"But it'll give you a place to direct them when they call," I say. I read over the statement one more time, just to make sure it would be Vin-approved.

Drenaline Surf would like to welcome Kale Nakoa to our roster of sponsored surfers. Kale hails from the North Shore of Oahu in Hawaii and grew up surfing classic surf spots like Pipeline and Back Door. His love for the sport and his surf-immersed spirit is exactly what Drenaline Surf is about and what Shark McAllister lived for. We're excited to have him on board as we move forward in the surf community.

At Drenaline Surf, we understand following your passion and chasing your dreams. It's the essence this company was founded upon and the ultimate belief of the McAllister family. We were saddened to see Vin Brooks leave the company last month, but we understood his desire to follow his passion in mechanics and take on a new opportunity in a field that he enjoyed. With this departure, a door has been opened for our new manager, Jace Hudson, to join the Drenaline Surf family and carry on its legacy.

We're excited to grow and evolve in the upcoming months and will announce all of our future projects soon.

– Haley Sullivan, Public Relations
(Haley.Sullivan@DrenalineSurf.com)

I submit the statement on our website and hope that all questions will be directed to me instead of Jace or – God forbid – Joe's house.

"That's all we can do for now," I tell him. "If anyone calls wanting a statement or a comment, tell them that our official press release is on our website and give them the web address. Say nothing more, nothing less."

Jace nods a few times, like his brain is still trying to absorb the insanity that is unfolding before us. "Thank you," he finally says, his voice somewhat low. "This is a far cry from the music store."

I push the office chair back and stand. "It'll get better. We're in a transitional phase, like Joe said," I tell him. "Now that we've averted the media crisis, I'm going to let you resume inventory control."

I walk out to the main room, hoping to steal Topher away for a few minutes to ask him how he knew about Kale's sponsorship before anyone else. I know Joe told him, obviously, but he couldn't have known for long. Topher couldn't have kept it from Miles if he had.

Logan intercepts me, though, before I reach the front counter.

"Hey, I sort of need to talk to you," he says, looking around sheepishly. It's like he doesn't know his place here. Actually, he probably doesn't.

"Is everything okay?" I ask. I remind myself to smile, to be warm and friendly. I've had a sour taste in my mouth about his arrival simply because everyone else felt offended by his entrance to Drenaline Surf. They accepted me. They somewhat accepted Colby. Logan deserves his chance too.

He shrugs. "I just…I need to talk to you about my career or image or whatever it is," he says. It's not the first time I've heard that line. "I'm tired of my name being dragged around like I'm some kind of victim. You're the damage control person, so can you fix it?"

Of course, I can fix it. I can more than fix it. I don't think Logan even realizes his own potential. If he's as great a surfer as Vin said he is, then he's the full package. He's marketable. He's someone you want on magazine covers. He just needs a team to back him, and he's not getting any of that here. My loyalty forever lies with Colby, but I'm not going to be one of

51

those people that article talked about. I won't give Logan the short straw.

"Let's go for a drive," I tell him. "We need to talk some things over."

"This is a hidden little gem," Logan says, dropping his shades over his eyes. He wears Oakleys, just like A.J. "How did you find it?"

"Colby brought me here once," I say, stepping onto the pier. "It's where he comes to think, to get away from the crowds and the craziness. Tourists don't really know about this spot. They're all out on The Strip. The pier is great there, but this one is more Zen."

I cringe upon the use of the word Zen. I can't believe it even came out of my mouth. I swallow the lump in my throat – and the memories of my ex-boyfriend – and focus on the matter at hand – Logan's career.

"I know I should ignore the tabloids and gossip sites," Logan says as we stroll along. "I have a terrible habit of Googling myself, but most of what I see are things I wish I hadn't. Even with all that's happened, Colby still has a huge following. People like Miles because he's edgy, and your boyfriend is crazy popular online."

"Really? I didn't know that," I lie.

But the truth is, I totally know it. During those sixty-three hours after the awkward kiss-and-run incident, I searched Topher's name online a few too many times. I wanted to see what people were saying about his sponsorship. I wanted to read the surf forums and see who was excited about it, who thought he deserved it.

Instead, I found a ton of girls who thought he was hot, who were bummed that he had photos posted of himself with Emily and me, and who basically wanted to be his surf girlfriend. It was all about Topher Brooks, not Drenaline Surf.

No one cared about Shark's legacy and how he was like Topher's second brother. No one cared that Vin was gone and Topher was a wreck over it, even if he tried to hide it. It was all about Topher, in a sense that wasn't even Topher as we all know him.

Topher had just landed his dream surf deal with his dream sponsor yet the only thing that mattered was that he was swoonworthy? Poor Alston had to sit through my hours of panic that people only saw Topher as a hot guy and not a professional surfer. I'm not sure if it was the possible girlfriend who was panicking or the PR girl panicking. I'll stick with the PR girl.

"I just don't want to be *that* guy, you know?" Logan says, pulling me back in. "I want to be known for surfing, not being an outcast. I want to do what Drenaline Surf was meant to do – continue Shark's dream. I know I never met the guy, but I felt like I did, you know?"

He gives me the detailed story about his journey to sponsorship, the story that Vin never elaborated on. Logan's dream to move to the west coast is what triggered his search of surf companies in California.

"I figured maybe I could transfer out here with a job, but none of the Florida stores had chains out here. I think they are all just too small. They can't compete in this area," he says. "I was browsing websites when I saw Drenaline Surf's site. I didn't think much of it at first. Just another surf site. But then I clicked on the 'about us' section and saw Shark's picture and read the story about him. It just hit me."

He tells me about his initial e-mail to Vin and how nervous he was sending it. He inquired about job positions and if Drenaline Surf was hiring.

"I'm not sure if he was honored or just freaked out by the whole thing," Logan says. He looks out across the water, like he can see the memories playing out on a large screen in front of him. "He was chill, though. He asked about who I was, what my ambitions were, why I wanted to move to California. So I was honest with him. I wanted to be a pro surfer, and I needed a surf-rich environment. But Drenaline Surf felt right compared to the bigger stores. I felt like it was based on something real."

Shortly after, Vin flew out to Florida to meet him, checked out some of his surf clips, spent a few days talking with him, and ultimately decided to sign him. Logan didn't even know until Vin flew him out to Crescent Cove. I crack a smile that I knew before Logan did. I was in that loop.

"But it was different after I got here," Logan says. "It wasn't a warm welcome to the Drenaline Surf family. Not even close. I mean, I won the Sunrise Valley Tournament, and I don't think one person congratulated me on it."

That's a day I'd personally like to forget.

"In my defense, I was fired from my job and broke up with my boyfriend that day," I say, even though it's a cop out. I wasn't happy that Logan won, either.

He shrugs. "Yeah, that day kind of sucked for everyone," he says. "There was so much drama with Vin and Topher and then Colby's parents. I don't know why I expected anyone to care that I won."

My heart sinks into my stomach like an anchor, except it doesn't stay planted. Instead, it sort of drags around in my gut, carving pain and sorrow into my being so I can't forget this moment later. We've really screwed this guy over. He came out here with big dreams and a lot of hope, and we've steadily been crushing every single moment of it, as hard as we can. It's not like anyone's invited him to hang out or tried to get to know him. I haven't even talked to him once about his career plans, even though I know exactly what Topher, Miles, and Colby all want individually.

"We screwed up," I admit, pushing my hair back behind

my shoulders. "But we're going to fix this. Who do you want to be? Tell me what you want, and let's make it happen."

He forces his sunglasses up into his hair. "I want to be Colby Taylor," he says, causing my jaw to drop to the ocean bottom. "Without the drama, obviously."

"Say that again," I say.

He laughs. "He has a huge following. People are excited to watch him surf. And aside from the mess with his parents, he seems to be well-liked. Ocean Blast Energy likes him. Shaka Magazine praises him. People turn up to see him surf, drama or not," he says. "I want that. I want to excite people. I want to be one of those surfers you either love or love to hate. And you know, I want to give back to the community and stuff."

He reminds me of a beauty pageant contestant – highlighted hair and a perfect tan, camera-worthy smile, and what seems to be a genuine personality. Of course, then they like to throw in that line about world peace or ending world hunger.

"And how do you plan on giving back?" I prompt him. I wait for a few stammers or half-answers, but he surprises me.

"I've always wanted to work with the sea animal conservation, like saving sea turtles. They're my favorite animal, and there are more of them here than in Florida," he explains. "I like all that environmental, go-green kind of stuff. I don't eat as clean as Colby does, but I have more in common with him than he realizes. Oh, and surf lessons. I've love to give surf lessons."

Surf lessons. How freaking genius! That's something Drenaline Surf hasn't offered in the past. It'd give people an experience rather than an item they bought on vacation. They'll remember the brand. They'll remember the surfers. It's priceless – for a price.

"If we started up a program, like if we could team up with some of the tourist venues or trip planners, would you be willing to help with a strategy for how to manage surf lessons? Like help head the program?" I ask.

"Are you kidding? I'd do it in a heartbeat," Logan says, his eyes wide and surprised more than excited. "Tell me when and where. I'm in."

CHAPTER 9

"This is fucking horse shit," A.J. shouts, slamming the oven shut. "I'm not doing it. I'm not fucking doing it, and he can fire me, and I'm done. I don't care. I want Vin back."

None of us react because A.J. has been saying the same thing for the last half hour. Reed pushes him aside to check the boiling noodles, and Alston makes a remark about not letting the garlic bread burn. But A.J. isn't really here tonight.

"Haley, you have to do something about it," A.J. demands. He leans against the countertop of the kitchen bar, staring across at me. "I can't call them. Jace is crazy."

I don't dare tell him, but I can see both sides of the issue. A.J. is Drenaline Surf's store manager. He needs to be the professional I know he can be and just make the call. But on the flip side, he's my best friend and his safe haven was destroyed to make way for a hotel. I totally understand his unwillingness to call them and make business deals.

"They're the only ones willing to partner with us right now," I tell him. "With all of tabloid crap, people are skeptical. They don't want to promise something we can't deliver, and seeing Miles on crutches and Colby's parents on TV really puts a few dents in the plan."

Alston takes the bread out of the oven while Reed douses the noodles with spaghetti sauce. They humor me with their ease of continuing dinner without a second thought to A.J.'s outburst in the kitchen, right in between them.

A.J. shakes his head. "They tore down my carnival," he says, a hint of desperation in his voice. "That place was my home. And now there's a big ass white hotel there with a zillion fucking flower beds because they're the Florence Gardens Inn. They took my house of mirrors for flower gardens."

But Florence Gardens Inn is the newest establishment in Crescent Cove. They're looking to build business. They want epic deals that hotel guests can't ignore. Why stay at the Crescent Inn when you can get a package deal with specials from Drenaline Surf and Strickland's Boating? I mean, I'd stay there…without telling A.J.

"Dude, I'll call if you'll shut up," Alston says. He bites into a piece of bread that he's impatiently waited for. "I'm pretending to be you, though."

"You still have to go to the meeting," I tell A.J. "If they agree to meet with us and sign a contract, you're going to fake it like the rest of us."

I may just manage the surfers' careers, but I refuse to let A.J. fail out of holding a grudge. I don't like it either, because of A.J., but Vin gave him an opportunity to lose the stereotype and make something of himself, and I'll be damned if he fails.

The next morning, Alston has formally arranged for a meeting with Florence Gardens Inn. Unfortunately, he's not going with us because he's under the command of Emily and her super training skills. Hopefully, between Jace and me, A.J. can be somewhat reined in.

I watch Alston ring up the next sale while Emily digs around in the inventory for new surfboard leashes. They seem to have it under control. I wonder if I can slip A.J. away for a while to prep him for the meeting tomorrow. Maybe we can grab Reed for lunch and have him play the part of the hotel manager. A.J. needs a practice run so desperately.

I turn to A.J. to suggest a trial run, but the bell dings over the door, drawing my attention back to the center of the room. Topher has newspapers in his hand. Miles is booking it on his crutches to keep up with Topher's pace. I'm actually impressed at his speed.

"So, we sort of have more problems," Topher says,

actually laughing through it. "It's crazy. Like totally ridiculous."

He slides the newspaper over the counter. A photo of us from the seahorse celebration is on the front page. I catch the words 'cult' and 'public relations' before I shove the paper away. My hands literally shake with nervousness about what's being said. I can't even read it.

"I can't," I say, stepping back toward A.J., who braces my unsteadiness. "What is this?"

Alston grabs the paper before Emily can and skims the article. "It says Drenaline Surf is an incest-ridden cult," he says.

He doesn't crack a smile. If anything, he looks disgusted and confused.

"It talks about how you dated Vin and now you're with Topher," Alston continues. "And that you work for Drenaline Surf, 'keeping it in the family' as they put it. It mentions Emily and Miles too. People are actually calling you guys Haler."

Haler? What the hell is a Haler?

"Dude, we have a ship name," Topher says. He's excited about this. How in the hell is there any way he can be excited? This is more damage. Does he not care that Drenaline Surf is being dragged down even more every time one of these things goes to press?

Miles shakes his head. "Haler is fucking stupid," he says. "It's like an inhaler or...some other stupid shit. Like a redneck saying 'halo' or something. You know, like some angel has its haler on crooked."

Miles's attempt at a southern accent is horrendous and thankfully hilarious. I guess it could've been worse. We could've been Tophey.

"What would we be?" Emily asks, propping her elbow on the counter and resting her chin on her fist. "Emiles? Em-uh-less...or E-miles? Em-iles? Ugh. Forget it. We suck. We can't compete with Haler."

Alston clears his throat. "It's bad, you guys. They mentioned Topher and Miles being best friends since forever ago. And that Haley and Emily hang out together. It's only a matter of time before they bring up the fact that A.J. and I are your roommates."

I hadn't thought of that. They'll pick us off, one by one. The only one who may be safe is Reed because he doesn't work here, but his parents gave Shark this lot to build on. Mr. Strickland helped Colby get a top-notch attorney. Reed drives Shark's old Jeep. And he lives with us. The connections are bound to come out sooner or later.

After taking a deep breath, I move forward and squeeze in between Emily and Alston. Pictures from my Instagram account are on the page. There's a photo of Emily and Miles as well. She Snapchatted it to me about a week or so ago before she posted it to her Facebook account as well.

"Make your accounts private," I tell her. "Now."

I grab my own phone from my pocket and immediately start updating my privacy settings. While I log in and hide my life, I lecture Miles and Topher about what they can and cannot post. No more girlfriend pictures. No more party pictures. Be professional. Be surf-related.

I can't believe I'm actually having to PR my own relationship. And my friends' relationship. This is outright ridiculous.

"Heeey…" Alston says, dragging out the word. "There's a name on here. Carson? Do you know a Carson?"

My mind rolls through its internal book of contacts, but I can't place it. It sounds somewhat familiar, but it's just not coming to me.

"G. Carson? Does that help?" Alston asks.

Topher inhales sharply. "Greg Carson!" he says too loudly. "He's the Liquid Spirit guy who wanted to sign me."

That's it. That's exactly how I know the name. We met him in Sunrise Valley. He offered one hell of a deal for Topher – a deal we never followed up on.

I lean closer to the newspaper. "Is he quoted in this? Did he say something about us?"

"No," Alston says, shaking his head. He points to the byline. "He wrote the article."

CHAPTER 10

Miles yells at Topher to 'Go left! No – right! Left, fucking left!' while I reread Greg Carson's slander for the hundredth time. Alston laughs hysterically when Topher's racecar crashes into a light pole and spins in circles. Miles curses, and Topher asks for a rematch. Obviously, video games are still most important in this household.

Reed sits next to me, glancing at my phone every few seconds to see if I'm still on this same site. I can't help it. It's like I can't look away. I feel like, maybe, if I read it enough, I'll find some hidden clue as to why Liquid Spirit would do this to us.

"Haley, let it go," Reed says, waving his hand in front of my phone. "You can quote that article by now. New sentences aren't going to magically appear."

I close the article and put my phone down. "I just want to know their motive," I tell him. "If we can get ahead of them, we can stop them."

Reed looks at me with sympathetic eyes and a half-smile. I know he thinks I'm crazy. I sort of want to shake him and scream at him. He doesn't work at Drenaline Surf. He's not the one who is supposed to make their image look good, no matter what. I feel like I'm failing Shark and I'm failing Joe and I'm failing the store. I'm failing its surfers and its legacy. I'm just failing.

There's a rattle on the window pane of the kitchen door. Kale invites himself in, with Emily not far behind him. I'm glad to see them. We need some cheerfulness around here. Kale jumps into the video game fest with Topher and Alston while Miles breaks away to see his girlfriend.

I stay right where I am, planted next to Reed and a few feet away from A.J., who hasn't said a word through all of this.

"Alright," Reed says, giving in. "Let's talk motive. Why would Liquid Spirit come after Drenaline Surf?"

"Me!" Topher shouts. He turns around and smiles all too happily. It makes me laugh.

But all of this for Topher? Why drag Colby's parents into it? Why sue him? So much of it doesn't make sense. Liquid Spirit doesn't need the money. They proved that when they built the most massive surf shop in California.

"Okay, Topher is an option," I admit. "Maybe they're scorned, but they don't need the money. Topher would be a pride thing. Who would sell them information?"

The room is quiet for a moment, aside from the sounds of screeching tires and revving engines on the TV screen. Then Kale says it.

"Dominic."

The puzzle pieces begin to fit. He has all the motive in the world. He didn't get signed by Drenaline Surf. He was somewhat kicked out of the Hooligans. He flunked out of college. He arrived back shortly around the time Colby's parents showed up, and it was *his* party that Colby went to and ended up on the Wall of Shame because of. He even invited Colby there to 'get his mind off of things.' It could easily have been a colossal ploy to start unraveling Drenaline Surf, surf leash by surf leash.

"Where is he now?" I ask, hoping someone actually knows so I can track him down, kick his ass first, and ask questions later.

"I heard he's in Indonesia," Miles says from across the room. He hobbles away from Emily to fill us in. "His dad sent him on a surf trip to get more experience, surf all the massive waves of the world. Fucking lucky bastard."

Kale nods. "I heard something about that. He was in Hawaii too, which pisses me off. That asshole doesn't deserve to surf my home breaks," he says. Then he shakes his head, actually mad about it, which is unlike Kale's easygoing nature. "My cousins sent me pictures from the last swell that came in. Amazing waves. I can't believe he may have been out there surfing it instead of me."

I toy around with Dominic's motive. Does he just want to bring us down because he's not part of us anymore? I can't see him caring that much. His dad can send him around the world to surf anywhere. He can get noticed at any given moment. Vin even said that Dominic was a great surfer, so he could easily grab sponsorships. Maybe that's what he's after – a Liquid Spirit sponsorship. The more he tells them about us, the closer he gets to signing the deal. He has the right connections here to find out what's happening at Drenaline Surf. Crescent Cove isn't *that* big. It's still an 'everybody talks' kind of town.

"We win, though," Topher says. "We all have each other, and we have Drenaline Surf. Who cares if Dominic is in Hawaii or Tahiti or wherever?"

Everyone nods in agreement, and another racecar takes off.

The chandeliers sparkle above us, casting tiny dots of lights on the white marble flooring. I inhale and exhale, as steadily as possible, keeping my legs crossed so maybe my nervousness won't show. *Be a professional, Haley. Fake it for today.*

"Will you stop stressing out?" A.J. whispers next to me. "You're making me nervous, and I'm already sweating."

I don't mean to laugh, but A.J. is so out of his element today. He wears khaki pants – that Alston had to iron for him – and a button-up white shirt that his tattoos still show through because it's thin. But he made the effort to look like a professional today, and I'm proud of him for it.

Jace, on the other hand, looks like he's done this a million times as he stands at the check-in counter of Florence Gardens Inn announcing our arrival.

"Fucking chandeliers," A.J. mumbles under his breath. "You know, there used to be giant tea cups sitting around here."

His eyes glaze over with nothing short of red anger. Instead of teacups and crazy mirrors, this place is now full of live plants, beautiful flowers, and fish tanks full of brightly colored salt-water fishes. If they'd replace that store-bought painting with some of Shark McAllister's photography, this place would be spectacular...for a hotel that destroyed my best friend's sacred grounds. On second thought, they don't deserve Shark's pictures.

Jace looks over and motions us toward him. The girl behind the front desk leads us to an office with a huge back glass rather than a wall. Whoever sits across from the manager has a perfectly gorgeous view of the beach. What a marketing strategy.

"Hi, I'm Jace Hudson. We're with Drenaline Surf," Jace says, stretching his arm across the desk to shake hands with the hotel manager. He quickly introduces us, making sure he adds our business titles behind our names, and we take a seat.

"I'm Margaret Pearson," the lady across the desk says. "It's so nice to meet you all."

Something about her strikes me down instantly. She's an older lady, maybe in her early sixties, and she's dressed in a suit that could've come out of Colby's mom's wardrobe. Her lipstick is a bright shade of coral, and I'm pretty sure Emily would have something to say about how it's the wrong shade to wear with that ugly tan pantsuit.

She folds her hands and speaks before Jace even has a chance to slide the Drenaline Surf brochure across her desk.

"We're all so honored that a longstanding local business would reach out to us for a partnership, and while we think it'd be a great source of business for both of us, I'm afraid we have a few concerns," she says.

Damn. This lady doesn't play. I'm sure she's seen the local news. The gossip mill around Crescent Cove is on a constant spin cycle. I'm prepared, though. I can defend the ordeal with Colby's parents. I can carefully word a rehearsed speech about Vin's departure. I can even BS some line about how we're hoping this will help us expand and allow us to branch out and find new talent. Go ahead, lady. Throw it at me. I've got this.

"I believe that there are always two sides to every story, so I haven't paid any mind to the things being said around town," she informs us. "However, one thing has been brought to our attention that I don't believe your public relations department can weave into a misunderstanding."

Jace clears his throat. "What exactly are you referring to?" he asks.

Her eyes shift to A.J. and then back to Jace. "I hate to have this conversation right here, but it's been brought to our attention that your manager has a criminal record," she says.

Oh, hell no. I know this crazy bitch didn't just go there. How in the hell did she even find out about that? A.J.'s record is sealed. He was under eighteen. Even the idiotic charges from Topher's joyride were dropped because there were no grounds for an arrest.

A.J. jumps up from his chair before my brain even finishes processing this information. He kicks the chair back behind him.

"I don't have a criminal record," he says, pressing both palms against the edge of her fancy oak wood desk. "But I'll let you know damn quick that if you want to talk about my record, we can sure as hell create one right here and now."

I stand and grab his arm, unsure of what I'm going to do if he actually decides to lunge for this woman.

"Let's go outside," I tell him, giving him a mild tug.

He pulls his arm free from my grasp, though, and leans forward. "You don't know what you've done coming in here," A.J. says, never taking his eyes away from the manager. "You and Florence and whoever the fucking hell you brought in here, you're all going to regret this. You will regret ever building on my grounds!"

This! *This* is why A.J. didn't want to come here. *This* is why he didn't want to make the phone call or be the manager for this meeting. As much as I hate that this is happening, I'm so glad Jace is here to see firsthand that there are certain lines you just can't cross with A.J. Gonzalez, and this was one of them.

I push him back away from the desk, but I don't dare speak. Instead, I push him toward the door in a crazed hurry, hoping the wild animal glare in his eyes will fade once we're outside and away from these shiny marbled floors.

The sunlight dips down and swoops under the canopy of palm trees, shedding just enough light onto A.J.'s face for me to see the pain written on his skin.

"Are you okay?" I ask. It seems like we all ask that a lot these days.

He shakes his head. "I lost it. I'm sorry. I completely fucking lost it," he says. He looks down, still shaking his head, like he's not quite sure what happened in there.

The same words continue to run together as he speaks – he lost it, he's sorry, he just lost it, he's sorry, Jace is going to kill him, and he's sorry.

"Fucking Pittman," he mutters. He balls his hand into a fist but stops before he actually punches anything around us. "How is this happening to me? I'm finally doing everything right, and this is the shit I get for it?"

I comb through the recent days in my mind, checking each file for any type of clue as to how this actually happened.

Why would someone inform Florence Gardens Inn about A.J.'s past? It doesn't even matter if he had a juvenile record. That thing is sealed. It's over and done.

"You think he did it?" A.J. asks.

"Who?" I question.

"Pittman," he says, as if it's the obvious answer. "I bet he warned them about me. Probably said I'd show up over here and act a fool because of where they built. They're probably in there calling him right now. Got him on speed dial. He's just waiting for me to lose it so he can haul me in and make it permanent."

I never, ever thought I'd say it, but I actually hope it was Pittman this time. At least then I could just blame it on his hatred for A.J. and his need to bring my best friend down. But this isn't the work of Crescent Cove's finest officer. Everything inside of me knows better.

"I don't think so," I admit, unable to look A.J. in the eye. "Whoever did this knew we were coming today to talk to them about a partnership. I think it's the same person who is trying to run Drenaline Surf through the mud. Liquid Spirit or Dominic or whoever it is behind all of this. Colby's parents maybe? I don't know. But I really don't think this was Pittman. I think this is related to the bigger picture."

When Jace finally exits the hotel, he's much calmer than I expected him to be. Even Vin would've laid into A.J. for saying the things he did in there. It wouldn't have mattered if they were in the wrong.

"Let's get out of here," Jace says, unlocking his truck. He gets into the driver's side seat and cranks up, his face serious the entire time.

"I'm sorry," A.J. says from the backseat.

Jace shakes his head and glances behind him before backing out of his parking spot and burning rubber in the newly paved parking lot.

"Fuck them," Jace says. "That bitch had the nerve to say she'd hold a signing for Logan or 'one of the other wholesome boys' as long as A.J. wasn't on the premises. Then she offered to put brochures in their lobby."

I wait with baited breath to hear if he actually agreed to this. I know we need some good publicity, but I won't stand for it at the cost of A.J.'s reputation.

Jace shakes his head again. "I told her I should've trusted A.J.'s instinct from the beginning and never even attempted to do business with them. I said that Drenaline Surf didn't need to be associated with a company like that. Then I thanked her for her time and left."

A.J. leans forward, in between the front seats. "So you're not mad at me?" he asks.

Jace smirks. "Well, you probably shouldn't have screamed the word 'fucking' in there, but hell – fuck it. I'm with you. I've got your back," he says.

And with that, Jace wins the award for best boss.

CHAPTER II

A media circus awaits us at the new location. TV crews, media vans, and reporters hover around waiting for the big announcement. They probably think this is going to be a press conference where we allow the media vultures to pick apart what's left of our reputation and dignity. They're here hoping to get the scoop on Colby's parents, Logan's ostracism, Vin's departure, or possibly even A.J.'s criminal record. They'll probably be disappointed to learn that we're opening a board shop.

Jace, Topher, and Kale help set up the podium and a bright red ribbon for the ribbon-cutting ceremony. Jace connects the sound system, and my heart breaks a little bit when I see how much more comfortable he is doing that than he is standing as Drenaline Surf's man-in-charge. Even though the music store hasn't officially closed down, they're only open three days a week, and they have a 'last day' set in stone.

"So, do we just stand here and look good?" Alston asks. He and A.J. match in their Drenaline Surf polo shirts and khaki pants. Alston definitely looks more professional, though.

"Yes," I say. I push my sunglasses up into my hair. "Do every single thing you can to make Drenaline Surf look good."

I remain close to my manager roommates to avoid being asked questions by the media. This isn't the moment for a press statement. Luckily, they keep their distance, talking among themselves, most likely guessing what our big news may be.

Soon after, Joe, the mayor of Crescent Cove, and the chief of police gather around the podium. The mayor welcomes everyone and thanks them for coming out today to join us for a special occasion. The chief of police follows, instructing the media to hold all questions until the end of the presentation to avoid any chaos.

Then Joe takes to the podium. He repeats the mayor's thanks before speaking.

"Many of you knew my son Jake and watched Drenaline Surf rise from the ground up," he says. "What you may not know is that he always dreamed of expanding, opening another store, and hopefully having a board shop of his own. It saddens me that he did not live to see it happen, but I'm honored to be surrounded by such an amazing group of people who believe in Jake's dream and have worked hard to help continue the vision my son had."

An eruption of applause surrounds us. I skim the crowd to see a lot of Drenaline Surf regulars standing among the people. Looks like the media wasn't the only group interested in what we were doing next. Both Horn Island and Crescent Cove residents stand in the crowd.

"It's such an honor to announce that we'll be opening the very first Drenaline Surf Board Shop right here in Crescent Cove," Joe announces. "We will begin ground work and renovation this week and plan to open in the fall. Right now, I'd like to welcome a few people on stage who have helped to make this dream a reality."

He invites Rob Hodges onstage, along with Theo. Rob speaks briefly about his career as a professional surfer and moves along into the conversation about board shaping after his retirement. He then publicizes his plans to share his knowledge and wisdom with Theo to help Drenaline Surf branch out into the world of board shaping.

"I don't look at this as the end of the era of Rob Hodges surfboards but as the beginning of the era of Theo Rowell surfboards," Rob proclaims.

Theo stands awkwardly on stage next to his mentor while Joe takes the mic and asks Jace and Alston to come onstage as well, as the respective boss man and future board shop manager. Once they've gathered, the mayor presents Joe with a shovel. Camera flashes bounce off the old windows of *Mallard Brothers Automotive* as the media crews snap the moment that red ribbon is officially cut. A large sign is staked in the ground next to the site. The words 'Future Home of Drenaline Surf Board Shop' pop in big, bold letters.

"Looks official," A.J. says. "What do you think?"

I drop my shades back over my eyes. "I think I'm getting out of here before the media locates me for a statement on something that isn't board shop related."

As I make my way along the back of the crowd, keeping my eyes focused toward where my car is parked across the street in the sand, I hear Topher shout my name. I spin around as he runs toward me.

"Wait!" he yells out. "You have to see this. Come here. Where's A.J.?"

I lead him back around the crowd of people, most of who have dispersed and are lingering around discussing what kinds of boards they hope they can get this fall. A.J. stands off to the side of the stage. I know he's waiting on Alston, who is trapped in a professional moment of hand-shaking and smiles with the mayor.

"A.J.! Dude. Joe needs to show you something," Topher says, grabbing A.J.'s arm and not giving him much of a choice. "Come back here. To the back of the shop."

When we get around the building, Joe waits inside. Mechanical machinery is still installed, like the Mallard brothers thought maybe they'd be back to work on cars again. It's a good thing Vin isn't here or he'd want to open a mechanic shop instead.

"Mr. Gonzalez," Joe says, smiling like Topher does when he's excited. "I know you're not going to be at this location, but I thought you could appreciate this more than anyone else."

He talks about Shark's idea for the sign at the other Drenaline Surf store, how he knew he wanted a massive wave hanging over the door. It was the hardest part of the building process, but his son was determined.

"When we were thinking of opening another store, I wanted to do something different," Joe explains, talking with his hands. "I wanted something big, something memorable…but something Jake would've approved of. So, I was able to salvage a little something, and I was thinking of using this across the roof, after we have the business name painted across it, if that's okay with you."

A.J. shifts his eyes toward Topher and me. Then he shrugs. "Why would I care what you did with a sign?" he asks. "I mean, I'm not trying to be rude or anything. I just don't see why *my* opinion is the one that counts."

Joe points a finger at him. "Oh, but you will," he says. "Topher, can you help me remove that tarp?"

Joe nods toward the item on the back wall. Topher walks down to the other end of whatever is hiding under the blue tarp. He grabs the corner of it and peeks behind.

"Holy shhhhh…Joe! This is amazing!" Topher hollers out. He bounces on the back of his flip-flops, unable to contain his excitement, in such a Topher-like way.

They rip away the plastic hiding the board shop's future sign. But it's no sign. It's the turquoise dragon that Jace unhitched from A.J.'s pirate ship the night of the great carnival rescue mission. Its orange eyes seem brighter now, up close with the sunlight pouring in through the back door.

"If I recall correctly," Joe says, "Topher said something about it looking like a wave. And I thought to myself, how awesome would it be to have that thing hanging over a Drenaline Surf shop someday? Of course, with A.J.'s permission."

A.J. falls forward, taking in the dragon in front of him that matches the one inked onto his arm. "I can't believe you saved it," he says, almost in a whisper. "This is fucking incredible."

Joe laughs. "I'll assume you approve then?"

"One-hundred percent," A.J. says.

It's not even three hours later when it hits the internet. I sit at the desk skimming the article yet again, knowing there's no way I can keep it from reaching Theo. He keeps up with the surf world more than any of the Hooligans. He browses the forums and reads the articles. He can quote rankings of any surfer on the world tour at any given time of the year. I've always thought it was a great way for him to keep his mind busy, but now, I'm crumbling inside knowing he'll read this article.

"How bad is it?" Topher asks from across the desk.

We're supposed to be filling out the rest of his entry form for the competition in Sunrise Valley this weekend, but I can't even focus on the paperwork.

"They said Drenaline Surf only hired him because he can't keep a job anywhere else," I tell him. I don't care if it's true. People shouldn't say stuff like this.

"What else?" Topher knows me too well. He knows there's more.

"That he has a drinking problem," I say. I prop my elbows on the desk and bury my face into my hands. At least they didn't mention Shark's death.

"Hey, it's going to be okay," Topher says, making his way around the desk. He wraps his arms around me and nuzzles his chin into my shoulder. "We know that Theo is broken. We all understand why. But this is going to help him. People are gonna talk no matter what. We just have to keep doing what we're doing."

I don't press the issue. Topher is right. We just have to keep moving forward. This is just another attempt to get under our skins, to make us feel like we can't prevail.

"You're right," I say, looking up at him. "I'm going to ignore this one and hope it just goes away. Eventually people will get bored with this, right? I mean, there's only so much you can say about a company before people just get tired of hearing it."

"Exactly," Topher says. He reaches across the desk and signs the rest of his paperwork. "There. You're done."

I think Topher is about to say something else when Jace walks into the office and halts all conversation. It's after hours, but he asks us to join him in the main room before we go.

Emily, Miles, Kale, Theo, Colby, and Logan are all gathered around the front counter when we walk into the showroom of Drenaline Surf. I slide around the counter and stand next to Emily. Topher remains at my side.

"I just wanted to have a quick word with you guys about this weekend," Jace says, standing opposite of all of us. "We're going to Sunrise Valley, and every surfer on our roster is set to compete, except the injured. The media is going to be watching us with a close eye. People are going to try to provoke us. Liquid Spirit will be there."

Miles leans forward against the counter, and I realize he's crutch-less. I'd completely forgotten that he got his cast off this morning. I lean back to see that he's in a boot. That's a good sign. Hopefully he'll be back in the water in a few weeks. I know he's driving Emily and Topher crazy waiting to get back out there.

Jace continues. "As hard as it may be, we need to all just keep our mouths shut, focus on professionalism, and be the bigger people. They want us to lose our cool. They're waiting for the thing to write about us. So take these next few days to clear your minds, breathe easy, and just focus on surfing."

It's close to midnight in our living room when I'm telling A.J. about Jace's surfer meeting. Reed lounges in the chair across from us, his legs draped over the side. It's rare that we're all here and awake at the same time, so if it takes a midnight rendezvous to see my roommates, I'll deal with the sleep deprivation later. But we're still one man down. Alston hasn't rolled in yet.

"And then they pulled the tarp back and it was my fucking dragon," A.J. says, slinging his arm out in Reed's direction. "Like the one on my arm. The one from the carnival. Fucking bitches may have taken my land, but I got to keep my dragon."

Reed laughs and mumbles something about how he can't believe A.J. actually cursed out an old lady.

"I kinda wish I was at the other store now," A.J. says. "At least then I could look at it every day when I go to work."

"Then look at your arm every morning," Reed says. He chucks a pillow at A.J.

The screen door in the kitchen opens. It's quiet, like Alston is trying to sneak in, but he catches our stare the moment he's inside.

"Late night?" Reed asks, pulling his legs back over the side of the chair. He sits upright and looks into the kitchen.

Alston shrugs. "Yeah, I guess. I was out. No big deal."

"On a Thursday night?" Reed asks. "Where is there in the cove to go *out* on a Thursday?"

What happened to the whole 'you can party any time' theory that everyone has been preaching to me? I thought you could party any damn time in California.

Alston grabs a bottle of water from the refrigerator, takes a long gulp, and then twists the lid back on. He stares at us over the countertop.

"What are you now? My mom?" he asks Reed. "I was out, okay? You want to know where I was? Fine. I'll fucking tell you. I was at Tropics. Okay?"

Reed and A.J. are completely silent while I rack my brain to figure out where Tropics is. Is that a store? It can't be a store. Even around here, stores shut down at a normal hour. I don't think I've seen Tropics yet. It has to be on the other side of downtown.

Alston grabs the water bottle and walks into the living room. "Now, are we all okay or is there going to be a problem?" he asks, holding his arms out.

"No, we're good," A.J. says. Simultaneously, Reed shakes his head and says, "No problem."

"Good," Alston says. "I'm going to bed. I'll see you guys in the morning."

With that, he drags himself upstairs like any other night, leaving me alone with Reed and A.J. in the living room. I wait until I hear Alston's bedroom door click shut before I say anything.

"Okay, what the hell is Tropics?" I ask, still keeping my voice low.

Reed swaps a glance with A.J., almost asking who should answer this question. A.J. shrugs his shoulders, like he's unsure how to answer that question.

"It's a night club...bar...place," A.J. says. "I've never been. Not really my type of place."

I glance to Reed, looking for elaboration.

Reed inhales and nods. "Yeah, what A.J. said," he says. "It's a bar, but...it's a gay bar."

CHAPTER 12

I wait on the bar stool with a soy latte sitting in front of me next to a bag of cheese biscuits from the bakery. It was hell getting up before dawn to get dressed for the day and then making a trip to grab breakfast, but when Alston strolls downstairs, expecting everyone else to still be sleeping, it's worth seeing the surprise on his face.

"Morning," he says, easing up to the counter. He points at the latte. "Is that mine?"

"Mm-hmm," I hum. "I grabbed breakfast too, if you want biscuits."

He slides onto the seat next to me and laughs. "You're worse than I am," he says. He takes a sip of coffee. "Is this your way to buttering me up?"

I can smell his pineapple shampoo from here. At least he's close enough to latch my claws into if he tries to run.

I shrug. "Is it working?"

It better be working because this boy owes me answers. As much as he likes to insert himself into my personal business, it's time for him to get a taste of his own medicine. I bite into my biscuit to try and play casual, but Alston sees through me more than I like. He knows I'm waiting for him to initiate the conversation, and he's not going to give me the pleasure.

"Look, you're always in my personal business, so you owe me answers about yours," I tell him. "Start talking."

He stands, grabs his coffee, and then slips his phone into his pocket. "Do you want to ride to work with me?" he asks. "We can talk about it on the way."

I grab my biscuit and vanilla frappe, pick up my bag on the way to the door, and hurry to his passenger seat. I'll find another way back home if I have to.

He cranks his car and turns the radio down. "Where do you want me to start?" he asks. "I figure A.J. and Reed told you what Tropics is, and you can pretty much figure out why I go there, so what are your questions?"

I sip my milkshake-like drink, trying to figure out how I even begin to ask questions. Alston is supposed to be this big playboy who loves the ladies and can't settle down with just one of them. That was his reputation last summer when I met him. He was flirty and hot and batted his eyes at every girl on The Strip. He was showing off his tattoo and looking for any reason to go shirtless.

"You made out with my friend last summer," I say. "My female friend. For like, two weeks. What the hell? I'm so confused."

Alston grabs his sunglasses and puts them on. I wonder if it's really to block the morning sun or if he just doesn't want me to see the look in his eyes when he answers that question.

"I'm sorry about Linzi," he begins, staring ahead at the street. "I wasn't completely sure. I mean, I figured I was, but I thought, hey, this girl is pretty and she's fun, and if I like her, maybe I do like girls too. I really tried to like her. She was safe. She was leaving, and you guys were temporary. Well, you were supposed to be, anyway."

Oh, if Linzi knew, she'd castrate him. I haven't talked to her since moving here, but she's Facebook official with some guy she met during a summer course at community college. She posts a lot of pictures of them together, so I'm pretty sure she's not dwelling on Alston or the fact that I moved to California, but still. She'd be mad. She loves talking about the gorgeous Asian boy she had a fling with during a magical time in Cali.

"I wasn't trying to use her," Alston says again. "I really thought you guys would leave, like everyone else, and it'd never matter. I didn't want to test my sexuality with a local who I'd have to see again. And really, no one else can tolerate A.J., but when you did, I knew I'd have to entertain your friend for at least a week, so…I'm sorry."

I put my cup in the cup holder and turn to face him. "So your whole playboy thing was just a ruse?" I ask. "You just figured you could pretend to be a playboy, so you wouldn't have to admit why you didn't have a girlfriend."

He nods, like it's not even a big deal. And I guess, in a sense, it really isn't. Linzi was a two-week fling with no potential of lasting. He knew that all along.

"Hold up," I say, remembering Linzi's final moments in the cove. "What about that big fight you guys had? The one where you were all 'you can't just come into my life and leave' and all that?"

Alston exhales and glances out his window before turning into the parking lot behind Drenaline Surf. He parks his car, but he doesn't kill the engine.

"It was for show," he says, resting his forehead against the steering wheel. "See, this is why I didn't want you to know. I knew you'd have these questions, and it just makes me look like the biggest asshat in the world."

"No," I say, reaching over and putting a hand on his shoulder. "I'm not mad. I'm closer to you than I am to Linzi these days. She's moved on. She's fine. But are you okay?"

There goes that question again. Are any of us actually okay anymore?

Alston half-shrugs, which is even more hopeless than an actual shrug. Then he leans back against the seat.

"I wish I could just be open about it, but you can't here," he says. He turns his head toward me but doesn't move his body. "This sport doesn't allow it, and I don't want to cause Drenaline Surf to lose any business."

I shake my head. "This is California. People are all about free love and being who you are," I remind him. I can't believe he even thinks it's an issue. "You can totally be you."

He reaches over and pops open his door. He grabs his coffee, takes a sip, and shakes his head. Then he steps outside and waits for me to follow. I meet him at the trunk of his car.

"Surfing is the most homophobic sport out there," he tells me. His voice remains low, and he glances around to make sure no one is close enough to hear him. "Do you see any gay surfers? I mean, there's this one guy in Los Angeles who surfs the qualifying series, and he's blasted for dyeing his hair neon colors. He's not even openly gay, if he's even gay at all. You just can't do it in our sport."

He leans back against the trunk of his car and plays cool when Jace pulls into the parking lot. "Can we just leave this in our household until it needs to be public?" he asks.

I nod my head. "Just us," I tell him.

Deep within me, I pray that whoever is leaking info about Drenaline Surf doesn't get on to this secret.

CHAPTER 13

Saturday morning, Drenaline Surf is a madhouse. We hadn't even planned on being in town, much less being slammed with business, but the surf event that was supposed to happen in Sunrise Valley has been moved to our beach.

"So is the dude okay?" Topher asks, looking up at me from a box of T-shirts.

"I'm not sure. They haven't updated the public since he went in as critical last night," I tell him. "They've closed the beach."

Part of me doesn't even want Topher to surf today – or any of our guys for that matter. We all know that shark attacks happen, and surfers risk it every time they venture into the ocean. It's their natural habitat, not ours. But in the back of everyone's minds, it's something that happens on other beaches, in other cities, far away from anyone we know or love.

"Shouldn't you be down the beach putting on a jersey and getting psyched up to surf?" I ask, pulling the box of shirts away from him. "It's competition day."

"I know, but it's so busy here. They need help," Topher says. "I still love the store. It needs me right now."

I put the box aside and give him a tight hug. "You're precious," I say, trying not to laugh because he's so serious right now. "Emily, Alston, and Kerianne are handling it up front. They've got this. Go surf."

"Fine," he mumbles. He presses a quick kiss to my forehead before leaving through Drenaline Surf's back door.

I follow behind and peek outside, just to make sure he's getting ready. He walks over to his truck and pulls a board from the back. Miles lingers around in his boot while Topher waxes the board. I close the door and sift through the papers on Jace's desk to find today's itinerary. Everything is off course now that the event has moved here.

But even among the chaos outside, Crescent Cove feels magical today. The vendors are smiling along The Strip. Tourists are hanging out on the beach, amazed to see an actual surf competition. People from all over this part of California are hanging out on our sand, waiting to watch some epic waves go down in the next few hours.

The air smells of grilled hot dogs, and the waves are washing in a perfect breeze. For the first time in weeks, I feel alive out here, like I'm back where I was last summer, waiting for a magical moment to happen. Of course, back then I was waiting to find Colby, and things were kind of messy, but there was a sense of hope. There was still a dream to chase. I was on my way – and today feels like that again.

I stop on the sidewalk and take a deep breath of Pacific Ocean air before I head down to the Drenaline Surf tent to handle reporters and keep my surfers on schedule. Different surf companies are set up along the beach under tents of their own. Their surfers hang out, taking photographs with young groms who want to grow up and be surf stars just like their idols. Some guys are signing caps and surfboards. Some are out in the water for a quick warm up before the competition starts. The entire beach is buzzing with surf community energy.

As I make my way to the Drenaline Surf tent, I notice the hellish crowd of surf paparazzi at the tent next to ours. My stomach twists without even seeing the logo because I know it's Liquid Spirit. Who in the living hell thought it'd be smart to put them next to us?

I slow down, hoping to catch a piece of whatever is happening. I'd rather be prepared than walk into this blindly.

"...in hopes of expanding. Right now, we're adding local talent to our register, but we're actively seeking surfers from across the country. By the end of next year, we're hoping to be a global company with talent representing the surf world internationally."

I haven't seen the voice behind the statement, but I'm pretty sure it's Greg Carson. I skim the crowd, but I don't want to be too obvious. I'd know him if I saw him, but just the same, he'd know me as well. I still have that envelope he sent Topher hanging out in a box in my bedroom closet. I guess I should've declined the contract, but a bigger fish was frying at that moment.

That international line is going to kill us, though. We couldn't go global even if we wanted to. Drenaline Surf isn't that big, and we don't have any corporate giants trying to team up with us. If we hadn't landed the deal with Ocean Blast Energy back when Vin was making deals, we probably couldn't get them now. Luckily, they adore Topher, and even with the drama, they think Colby is amazing. I'm definitely pitching Logan to them soon. He's magazine-cover material.

"This sucks," Miles says as soon as I step under the tent. "I'm like the only one who isn't surfing today."

He slings himself down onto a chair. Selling Drenaline Surf T-shirts and last minute surf wax isn't his idea of a good competition. I know he's mad because he was out of the last one with a broken leg – and his replacement won the event – but I can't let him in the water with that freaking boot on.

No one wants to see you surf anyway.

I spin around, but I don't know which Liquid Spirit idiot said it. Topher is at my side immediately, staring them down like he could ram a surfboard through them.

"Step back," I say through my teeth. I turn and face him. "I know Miles is your best friend and you want to defend him, but you've gotta keep it together today."

Topher turns his back to the enemy's tent. "They piss me off," he says.

"And they're going to all day long," I remind him. "That's what they feed on. They want to get under your skin so you'll do something you'll regret."

He takes a deep breath. "I know. I'm going to down some Ocean Blast and wax my backup boards," he says.

He walks away before I can attempt any kind of comfort. He's like his brother in that sense. He wants to handle things his own way, in his own time. But I have to let him walk on this one.

At least we don't surf for a cult. I don't know why Colby gets all the magazine interviews when Logan out surfs him any day of the week. Why is Logan even surfing for them anyway?

I force a fake smile and try to tune out all the smartass comments being shouted our way. I let Jace's words of wisdom rush through my brain like a waterfall rinsing away the negativity. They're trying to provoke us. They want a scene. I'm able to drown them out when a guy with SurfTube asks if we have any upcoming projects, aside from the board shop. Logan is quick to come to my aid.

"We don't have an official schedule yet, but I've talked to Haley about maybe setting up a program where we can offer surf lessons to young groms or just people on vacation looking for an awesome experience with the ocean," Logan says, all smiles while he speaks.

"I'm a firm believer in giving back to the community, and the surf community has been so welcoming and inspiring ever since I moved out here," Logan lies.

I hate that he has to play this part for us. He's such a puppet, and I'm sure everyone can see it, but they can't prove it. I'm thankful for that.

"But I'm super stoked to be part of this," he continues. "I never had the opportunity to meet Shark McAllister, but I believe in his vision. That's why I wanted to surf for Drenaline Surf rather than a huge corporation. I wanted to be in a place that really focused on the heart of surfing, and I can't think of anywhere better than here to be."

Should I just turn in my resignation letter? This guy is better at PR than I am, and he didn't even have 'master manipulator' Vin Brooks to train him. Once the SurfTube guy has moved on to the next tent, I pull Logan aside.

"Were you a PR rep in another life?" I ask.

His face falls grim. "I'm so sorry," he says. "Did I overstep?"

"No," I say quickly. "You were just very much on point, like you'd been trained to say exactly the right thing in the moment."

He laughs. "I was on the debate team in high school. I had to learn to think on my feet. It's one of my few natural talents," he says.

Colby Taylor is such a fraud. That whole company is full of incest with their inner-circle dating. Isn't that Theo guy an alcoholic?

Logan's eyes meet mine upon hearing the remarks. I send him off to prepare for his heat. Then I glance at our neighbor's tent. The Liquid Spirit guys hover around the edge, staring over at our staff like they're waiting for someone to make a move.

They're close enough to make us uncomfortable but not close enough that we can complain to the beach security. It's like there's a literal line drawn in the sand, and they're toeing the edge.

I walk around the table of merch and find Jace. Something has to give. I can't keep the Hooligans at bay too long. It'll only take a few more jabs before Miles is hopping on his one good foot toward them to shove a literal boot up their asses.

"This is getting out of hand," I whisper. "They're going above and beyond to provoke us."

A.J. walks up next to me, just arriving at the tent, to see what's going on. And that's when the next insult comes our way.

"Look at the freaks they've got working for them," a guy shouts out. "Isn't that the guy who stays in jail?"

Jace shakes his head, letting A.J. know not to react. I'm surprised at how calm my crazy Mexican roommate is. It's like he's not even offended. He's probably heard it more times than I realize, though.

"I wish I still had my crutches," Miles says, pushing himself up off the chair. "I might not can walk, but I could beat the fuck out of some Liquid Spirit sons of bitches with those things."

"Sit down," Jace orders. "No one is beating anyone with anything, and you need to watch your mouth. You're representing Shark McAllister and Drenaline Surf."

Miles laughs. "And Shark would've already busted that motherfucker's face wide open."

Jace tilts his head and squeezes the back of his neck. You can tell that he hates to smile at Miles's comment, but he does.

"I like to think that Shark was on the path of growing up," Jace says. "He was still professional, and that's what we need to be. I'm posting myself up over here, between you guys and Liquid Spirit, so if you're going to jump someone's ass, you're going to have to get through me first."

Jace settles into his spot, still under our tent, with his back turned to Liquid Spirit. He folds his arms over his chest and stands like a bouncer at a club who refuses to let you in the door. He seems taller, and he's already six-foot-three. He's never looked dangerous before, but that close-to-his-scalp haircut and rugged jawline seem more defined now, more militant.

I can't believe they hired Shark McAllister's drunkass murderer.

And that's when it happens. Jace spins around, and his fist meets the guy's face.

CHAPTER 14

This definitely wasn't part of my training. Once the initial fist is thrown, an eruption of chaos and disturbance overflows from the Drenaline Surf/Liquid Spirit battle, like a volcano spewing the hottest of lavas over the sands. Jace pulls back, instantly realizing that he lost his cool, but it's too late now. The damage has been done.

Miles inserts himself into the madness, using his elbow like it's a lethal weapon, all while managing to balance on his one good foot. Kale darts past me in such a blur that his dark hair and perfect tan almost look like a CGI wolf-shift from a paranormal film.

Theo grabs Jace's shoulders, pulling him back from the madness. But there's a glimmer in Theo's eyes that scares me because I know he's flirting with that dangerous line between stopping the madness and joining the fight.

It's absolute pandemonium that I can't even think of stopping. Those few seconds between pushing and shoving, upturned tables, and flying fists and the eventual arrival of beach security feel like lingering moments of eternity.

Given, they got here quickly. Colby and Logan didn't even make it back to our tent in time to see any of it go down.

"What the fuck just happened?" A.J. asks, pushing through the onlookers who've been screaming 'FIGHT!' this entire time.

"Jace punched a guy," I say, my voice shaky. "We're so fucked."

"Whoa. Wha…What? *Jace*?" A.J. asks as security guards push themselves in between our two tents.

Jace grabs Miles and pulls him back, but he can't stop Miles from popping off at the mouth. The boy just keeps shouting.

Logan calms Kale down while Topher isolates Miles from the rest of the beach. At least about half of our Drenaline Surf team was somewhat composed. Then again, I doubt that makes any kind of difference because our boss threw the first punch.

The security team takes statements from Liquid Spirit first. Greg Carson hovers over every surfer and staff member as they speak, like he's overseeing the statements to make sure we're made to be the bad guys in this situation.

I keep my back turned to the crowd around the tents, hoping not to get caught in the crossfire. A girl from SurfTube is a few feet away, covering the story about a 'chaotic fight that broke out' between two rival surf companies. This just gets better and better. All of that great footage of Logan talking about surf lessons and giving back probably got deleted from the hard drives to make room for this crap.

"I can't believe I did that," Jace says, sitting on a box of Drenaline Surf merchandise. "I absolutely fucked us over. After all that preaching I did…"

This was truly the last thing I expected to happen today. I was prepared for gossip and smart remarks. I was ready for the lies and attempts to provoke us. I was more than ready to break Miles's other leg the moment he started hobbling toward someone ready to fight.

"What happens now?" Jace asks, looking up from the sand toward me.

"Well, we will probably be disqualified," I tell him. "We may even be banned from certain events in the future. They'll probably force us to leave the beach. And the usual media circus will have the ultimate tabloid party at our expense."

That's the worst that I can dream up, anyway. It's typical. I refuse to let myself dwell on the consequences of today. It's crazy how I went from super hopeful this morning to feeling like the world just crashed down on us. Today was supposed to bring us back to the heart of surfing. Now I might as well pack up our tent.

A security officer comes over to our tent and speaks with Jace first. I stick closely to them, to make sure I'm fully aware of what is said so it can't bite us later. I didn't even learn that trick from PR. I learned it from Colby Taylor.

"I just need you to be honest with me," the security officer says. "I'm getting statements from the other parties involved that you threw the first punch. Is this correct?"

Jace exhales, defeated. "Yes, that is correct."

"Because you initiated the fight, we've been asked by the Beach Marshal and event organizers that your team be disqualified from competing and all persons working for your company be escorted off the beach immediately," the security officer explains.

They allow us long enough to pack up all of our Drenaline Surf merch and bring the tent down, which may be even more embarrassing than watching Jace throw punches at another surf company. It's like the ultimate walk of shame bringing down that big blue tarp while people crowd around to watch like we're taking someone to an execution.

Jace keeps his sunglasses over his eyes, refusing to speak to anyone other than telling us where to load things in the back of his vehicle. I think he's kicking his own ass harder than Liquid Spirit could have even if they'd stood a chance.

"Let's just get this stuff back to the store," Jace says. "We'll unload in the back parking lot and just stack the boxes against the office wall. I'll handle the inventory side of it and restock later."

The security team follows us as we make our way back to the vehicles. I actually hear the clicking of camera lenses, capturing our disgrace to plaster across the internet, the gossip sites, the surf forums, and tomorrow's Crescent Cove tabloids.

I assign A.J. to Topher and Kale. Then I direct Logan and

Colby to keep a firm grasp on Miles. I can't watch all of them and maintain a professional image when I want to slip beneath the waves and float away. Luckily, half of our team is level-headed at the moment, while the other half are, well, Hooligans.

My 'just keep walking' mentality fades away quickly, though, the instant I see the blue lights in the distance. And those lights can only mean one thing – Pittman. I turn back to A.J., but I know he hasn't done anything to provoke the law. He wasn't even involved in the fight. There's no way this asshole cop is pinning this on him. I won't let him.

Pittman leans back against the patrol car, casually waiting as we approach the parking lot. Something about him reminds me of Vin. Maybe it's the dark hair and that piercing glare in his eyes. Or maybe it's the arrogance. He is winter meets warmth, sort of like biting into a gooey chocolate bar but realizing there are shards of glass inside. That's the vibe I get from A.J.'s favorite officer.

"Jace Hudson," he says, pushing himself off of the car and easing toward us.

"Alex," Jace says, no hint of emotion in his voice.

Alex? I guess I just never thought of Pittman actually having a first name. It's weird. It makes him more human, and I'm not quite sure I want to think of him as an actual person.

"I hate to do this to you," Pittman says, looking away from Jace. "Liquid Spirit is pressing charges, and we have to take you in. I asked them to let me do it."

Jace shakes his head and chokes out a dry laugh. I can't find any humor in this, but I think he's just truly over it. All of it.

"Can you give me a minute to get some things in order?" Jace asks.

"Of course," Pittman says.

Jace turns to me and pulls his wallet from his back pocket.

"You're going to have to go to the ATM to get bail money," he informs me. "I'll write down the PIN for you. Take my cell phone with you. Call Joe and tell him that I may have to borrow money from the safe if my bail is more than the ATM lets you withdraw. I can pay him back tomorrow."

He gives me his truck keys and asks me not to leave him in jail for too long. Then he walks back over to Pittman.

"Alright, let's get this over with," Jace says.

Pittman shakes his head. "I'm not cuffing you," he says. "I have more respect for you than that. I know you. These assholes are just doing this because they can. Just get in the car. The hell with policy."

I watch until Jace is secure in the back of the patrol car, amidst the camera flashes. Then I head to his truck so I can get the hell out of here as quickly as possible. The Crescent Cove police do a pretty good job of keeping the media sharks at a distance, but I know those zoom lenses are in high usage right now. This is the money shot for them. Jace in the back of a patrol car. I never thought I'd see the day. The only way it'd be more shocking would be if it was Reed rather than Jace.

"Haley!" I spin around when I don't recognize the voice. I fear it's a media fiend wanting a press statement, but it's Pittman. He walks toward me, ignoring the cameras that are following him from the required distance.

"There's a bank a block over from the station. It'll be easier to get to than the one near Drenaline Surf," he says. "I'm going to take my time on his paperwork and keep him in booking until you can get there. I'm not letting him see the inside of a jail cell. You can follow me out if you'd like."

I simply nod because I don't know what else to do. I don't want any favors from him, and I sure as hell don't trust him after what all he's done to A.J., but right now, I don't really have any other choice. I can't let Jace sit at the station any longer than he has to. So I get in his truck, I crank up, and I follow Pittman away from the premises.

Reed's Jeep sits in the parking lot of the police station when I arrive. He immediately darts out of the driver's seat and jogs toward Jace's truck when he sees me.

"What happened? I've been seeing all kinds of stuff on the news," Reed says.

I lock Jace's truck and glance around the parking lot. The last time I was here, Reed was with me. We were collecting A.J., Topher, and that same blue Jeep. That was just a month ago. How does it feel like it was another lifetime? I sort of wish my biggest problem was Topher joyriding to blow off steam from fighting with his brother.

"Someone referred to Theo as Shark's 'drunkass murderer' and Jace lost it," I say. "After all those lectures about professionalism, he threw the first punch."

Reed laughs, and I want throw a punch at him for even thinking for half a second that anything could be funny about this.

"You can take the boy out of the surf gang, but you'll never take the Hooligan out of Jace," Reed says. "I mean, he *is* one of them. And Theo's his boy."

And just like Jace did before his arrest, I laugh. The same exhausted, 'over it' kind of laugh. But in my case, it's so I won't completely break down here in the police station's parking lot. If I gave in to everything I'm feeling inside, I'd be an asphalt puddle right now, melting into the blackness under my flip-flops.

"How did you even know to come out here?" I ask.

Reed smiles. "A.J.," he says. "He called and said he didn't want you to have to deal with this alone and I was a better candidate to show up at the jail than he was. He's handling things at Drenaline Surf right now. Alston and Emily are there too, so he's got help."

I wish Pittman could hear all of this. A.J. isn't the guy he makes him out to be. But maybe Pittman isn't the asshole cop I've always made him out to be. He broke protocol in front of a ton of cameras today out of respect for Jace and allowing him to keep some of his dignity.

Reed walks into the station with me and makes small talk with the chief of police. They quickly discuss business and how Mr. Strickland has been before Reed tells him that we need to post bail for Jace Hudson.

While Reed handles the monetary side of things, another deputy takes me back to an office where Pittman sits at a desk pretending to fill out paperwork. Jace sits in the chair opposite the desk. It's a far cry from the day I came to pick up A.J. and Topher.

"Reed's posting your bail," I say, once the escorting deputy walks away. "A.J.'s handling the drama at the store. Joe is going to meet us there. He's okay, though."

Jace looks at his shoes for a few seconds, nodding along, clearly thinking about having to face Joe and try to explain what happened today. I've already given him the quick version, and he was more than understanding. He knows what Theo has been through. He seems to care more than anyone else, like he knows it's deeper than a usual depression or guilt trip. There's no way he could be mad at Jace for defending Theo.

Pittman looks at me. "Do you need an escort back to the store?" he asks.

I shake my head. "No one followed me," I tell him. "And Reed met me out here, so we're not alone."

I don't know why I even say it because Reed Strickland isn't exactly bodyguard material. We all learned that last summer when I realized he couldn't hide Colby to save his own life.

"Let's get out of here," Jace says, pushing his chair back

and standing. Then he halts and turns back to Pittman. He pulls a business card from his wallet. "Thanks for all you did today. If you need anything, here's my card. I'm obviously not at Strings and Starlight anymore, but my cell phone is listed on there. Let me know if you need help, seriously."

Pittman thanks him, they shake hands, and then Jace walks out with Reed and me like he wasn't just booked into jail. I guess Crescent Cove does whatever Crescent Cove wants – as long as you're not A.J. Gonzalez.

CHAPTER 15

Emily stares at the drive-in menu for longer than necessary, especially when I know she's going to end up getting a plain grilled chicken sandwich and a grape slush. If she's feeling a little rebellious, she may get a small order of tater tots as well.

"Are you sure you don't want anything?" she asks, glancing over her shoulder at me. She stretches her arm out of her window but waits before pressing the button to order.

"I'm sure," I tell her yet again. "I don't think I can stomach anything else today. No food. No drama. No more police station visits. I'm good."

As predicted, she goes for the plain grilled chicken sandwich. She upgrades her grape slush to a large but skips the tater tot rebellion. She digs through her car for loose change to pay the exact amount. She's eyeball-deep in her cup holder when she says it.

"Would you ever consider moving in with Topher? Like getting an apartment with him or something?" she asks.

Oh God. Please don't tell me he's working through Emily to feel me out. I know he doesn't really like living at Colby's house, and he doesn't want to move into Shark's old place, but I can't move in with Topher. We've just started dating, and that's a huge leap, and I love where I live. I don't want to leave my roommates. We're sort of perfect in our arrangement.

"No, it's waaaay too soon," I tell her, shaking my head for extra emphasis. "I need to be where I am. I'm good living with A.J., Alston, and Reed for the time being. I like having the guest house for me. Moving in with Topher would be too much too soon."

Emily laughs but doesn't have a chance to elaborate. She pays for her food and guzzles her grape slush like she hasn't had any hydration in a week. Once it's secured in her cup holder, she looks toward me.

"I wasn't asking about you and Topher in particular," she says. "Well, not really. I guess it was an example. Miles keeps mentioning how we should get an apartment, and I'm not sure if it's too soon or if it'll be all I hope it'll be."

"You'll need a second job," I tell her. "Not for rent or bills or anything. Just to feed the boy."

In between bites of her sandwich, she explains how Miles doesn't want to move back home and how he didn't really think out the whole 'move in with Colby' thing.

"Don't get me wrong. He loves the free surf spot and Colby's flat screen, but I'm so sick of hearing about organic food. Miles is freaking obsessed with it. It's all he ever talks about – how he can't understand how Colby survives or he'll call me and read the ingredients off and freak out that people actually eat whatever it is he's holding," Emily says. "I just want to go back to life when he loved pickles and breakfast burritos and didn't know that organic cereal exists."

As much as I'd love to assure her that Colby is in fact human and sometimes eats carb-loaded pastas and French fries, I don't because I know she'll tell Miles, and it's too funny to give him the satisfaction of knowing. That's a loop Miles can't be in.

"So I found this rental house in Horn Island," she says, drifting away from organic cereal. "I really like it. It needs some work, but they're willing to do rent-to-own, so I still have time to decide if this is my forever plan."

Emily talks about how she wants a turquoise kitchen with white cabinets. She also wants a white picket fence, or maybe a purple one, but she's not sure she can convince Miles to even let her have a picket fence at all.

"It's by the beach, though, so Miles could surf every day, even if it's not Hooligan territory," she says. "Or he could drive out to the rocks. It's this perfect little spot between the cove and the land of Hooligans. I haven't told him yet, though, because he'll do it just because I'm onboard with it. I don't want things to completely change if we move in together, you know?"

It's weird that Emily is the one needing convincing instead of Miles. He seems more like the uncertain type, the one who would hesitate about taking such a big step. Emily seems much more free-spirited.

"Why is he the one who's pushing for this?" I ask, out of sheer curiosity.

"Ever since he moved out of his mom's house, I think he's felt like somewhat of a nomad. I know he's only moved into Colby's house, but it's *Colby's* house. It's not home," Emily explains, in between bites. "He's always had this stability, even in Horn Island, that he can't seem to find now. I think he just wants something more solid, something to make him feel safe."

Miles had been so excited to move out of his mom's house and be on his own. But I understand the need for stability. I haven't had any since I got back to the California, and I can't help but hope this will all eventually slow down and feel like a normal life. There's enough excitement in the sport of surfing to keep me on edge. I don't need added drama.

Emily sighs and twirls the straw to the best of her ability in its crushed ice. "Okay, I have another question, and I want you to be real with me," she says. "Would you feel weird if Miles and I asked Topher to room with us?"

"Are you serious? Why would I be mad? I live with three guys," I tell her.

I'm not sure if she thinks I'd be jealous or offended or left out. Or maybe she's afraid people will talk or it could create a bad image for all of us. I don't know what she's concerned about, but I think it's probably a better idea than Miles and Topher living with Colby. The fact that they are still on edge about his intentions and questioning his truthfulness bothers me – even if I understand why and honestly can't blame them.

"You're sure it's not weird?" she asks again.

I nod. "Positive," I assure her.

She exhales. "Good. Miles likes having Topher around, and I think it helps Topher since Vin left, and he doesn't have to be– shit. I'm sorry. Awkward. Moving along."

It amazes me how people forget that Vin and I dated. Maybe it's because they didn't see us together for the majority of our relationship. I was in North Carolina and he was in California, and we had most of our relationship over phone calls, text messages, and a few scattered visits from him when my parents were cool enough to let it happen.

It actually really sucks that we fell apart *after* I moved out here. By then, my parents were out of the equation. We had all the freedom to see each other. We had every tool to make that relationship work properly.

But then I wouldn't be with Topher. Topher's the one who dreams of something bigger, who doesn't worry with all the mundane details of day-to-day life. That's the kind of person I need next to me. I need someone to balance me out. I need someone who understands the urge to rush off to the west coast because of some chewed gum and a paper star. I need forever chasers, and forever is something Vin couldn't foresee.

Not much is said as Emily crumples up her bag and drives around to a trash bin to toss it away. She fumbles through the radio stations, mentions liking this one song, hating another one, and screams at a car that just flew past her doing at least eighty miles-per-hour on the highway.

"Do you think Jace will be weird tonight?" she asks. "You know, since the arrest?"

He will most definitely be weird tonight. It's been a few hours, so he's had time to let the adrenaline rush wear off, but the only problem with that is now he'll be more concerned and worried about the aftermath. He's probably sitting in his office right now trying to think of how we'll handle the media once this blows up overnight. It's already hit SurfTube and the internet, but Crescent Cove's local gossip tabloid is at press right this moment. It'll be plastered up and down The Strip in the morning, decorating the newsstands right outside of Drenaline Surf.

"Jace can handle it," I say instead. I glance out the window to see dusk settling in above the ocean, wiping away the remnants of color among the clouds. "He's level-headed. He will find a way to downplay it or maybe just ignore it."

When we arrive at Drenaline Surf, I unlock the front door. Boxes are strewn around the main showroom, some overflowing on the floor. This is all we have to show for the competition today – merch that was crammed into boxes haphazardly and brought back to the store to go unsold.

Kale and Logan are already here. Logan looks up from a box of T-shirts and acknowledges us with a half-smile. Then he scribbles something down on the inventory form on his clipboard.

"Hopefully we didn't lose too much," Jace says from the office doorway. "Just grab a box and a control sheet. That's all I know to do."

Emily and I join in, documenting shirt sizes and colors so Jace can compare them to the list of items that left the store today. In the madness of punches and elbows today, it's been rumored that Liquid Spirit lost a lot of items due to thieves grabbing and running in the commotion. They don't seem to mind. Greg Carson even laughed on camera saying that it's free advertisement and 'maybe they'll like our products to enough to actually purchase them next time.'

It's easy for a corporation like Liquid Spirit to lose a few shirts and blocks of surf wax. We don't have that luxury. Every single T-shirt matters. Every surf leash, every board, every pair of sunglasses. Those are the things that keep this store afloat. That's what keeps our surfers in events. That's what lets Shark's dream continue, and it's hard as hell to keep going in a world that's all about the take and never about the give.

Fortunately, we have people like Kale and Logan who are so entirely grateful for their sponsorships that they spend their evening counting shirts for Jace when Kale could've been having an awesome beach luau at his house or Logan could've been…doing whatever it is that Logan does when he's alone.

Jace tells us to holler if we need him and shuts himself away in the back office. He doesn't seem to want to make eye contact with anyone tonight. I hope he's not in there banging his head against the wall for what happened today.

I grab a box from behind the counter and settle in next to Logan on the floor.

"You gave up your awesome Saturday night plans for this?" I ask, hoping he'll give me some insight as to what the hell he does around here.

"Playing online word games isn't as much fun as you'd think," Logan says, looking at the tag inside a blue Drenaline Surf shirt. "There are only so many words that rhyme with 'made.'"

"Shade, glade, fade, wade," Kale rambles off from across the room.

I wish I had never asked because Kale spends the next hour rambling off rhyming words for any random word he can grab from our conversations. At times, it's hilarious, but Kale's enthusiasm can be overbearing after a while, especially after the kind of day we've had.

It's shortly after nine o'clock when Logan calls it a night.

He says something about meeting a trainer in the morning for a work out session, but I don't bother with getting details. It does strike me as odd that only one of our Drenaline Surf surfers has a trainer. I guess that's what Logan's been doing since he hasn't been invited to hang out with anyone. He's been prepping to become a better surfer.

Then Emily asks the question that I refuse to ask myself. "Who meets with a trainer on a Sunday morning?"

Oh, why did she have to bring that to the surface? No one meets with a trainer on Sunday mornings, that's who. If he wanted to quit counting shirts or just go home and crash, he could've said so.

Kale laughs. "He just said that so he could go home and play online," he says. "He probably reads stuff about himself and then plays online poker or something to blow off steam. Word games? Really? C'mon. You guys didn't buy that, did you?"

For half a second, yes. But Kale is right. Word games and Sunday training sessions? I feel like such an idiot for thinking Logan may actually be this great guy and a good representative of Drenaline Surf.

"No way," Emily says. "Word games? I knew he was bullshitting the moment he said that. I'm still on the fence about him."

Suddenly, I am too. I can't imagine him trying to harm Drenaline Surf, but he fed me the perfect story about having never met Shark but believing in his vision. He played into the 'I want to be like Colby Taylor' game, which is sadly a way to connect with me, even if I hate admitting it. Did Logan play me for a fool? Was that all just a beautifully tanned poker face that I fell for?

And it clicks – poker.

The clipboard falls from my hands, and Emily and Kale jump at the sound.

"Sorry," I say, snatching it up from the floor. "What you said – online poker. Do you think Logan is gambling?"

Kale shrugs and shakes his head, like he isn't even sure where I'm coming from digging into his random offhand remark. Sometimes this boy is so dense.

"Think about it," I say. "If he's gambling, he needs money. He needs fast money. He's probably blown through the sign-on bonus for his contract. He's only won that one event since he's been signed. Do you think he's selling stories to the tabloids? What if Colby's parents are paying him off for info about their son?"

My brain may actually burst. Here I was blaming Dominic – with reason – for digging our graves. I even thought Greg Carson was heartbroken over losing Topher to us. This may have been an inside job all along, just like Colby said he thought it was.

"Haley, do you hear yourself?" Kale asks, cracking a silly smile. "We could turn this around on any of us. You and Colby could be painted as guilty as easily as Logan just because you're not from here. Hell, I'm not even from here. You're starting to think like those crazy gossip columnists you've been reading."

I laugh it off because I don't want Kale or Emily to know just how deep I've drowned in the PR nightmare that is Drenaline Surf. But if I'm going to get ahead of these media pricks, I have to think like them. Maybe then, I'll be one step closer to figuring out who is pulling us under.

CHAPTER 16

"Sixteen shirts, eight things of surf wax, and three surf leashes," I recount to Jace the next morning. I place the inventory control forms on his desk. "That's what we lost."

"That along with four entry fees, my bail money, and those little things I used to call my reputation and dignity," Jace says.

He unfolds the front page of the Cove Gazette to show me the damage. It's in black and white, which I think actually makes it look harsher than it already does.

"I officially have a mug shot," Jace declares. "Can I just hang myself on the Wall of Shame next to Colby's coffee table meltdown?"

I haven't actually looked at that wall since the day Vin taped Colby's tabletop disaster to it. He seems to have added to it along the way, before his big departure. There's an article about Colby's parents with a photograph of Mrs. Burks. It's from the day of her arrival. She's on the beach with that large sunhat, hand over her heart, jaw dropped. How unbelievable staged.

"Personally, I think you've earned your spot," I say, reaching over for the tape dispenser.

Jace laughs, which eases some of the nervousness I felt when I woke up this morning. He's brushing this off. He's moving forward. That's the attitude we need right now.

"I bet Shark never imagined my mug shot would be on the wall of Drenaline Surf when he started posting photographs on the wall in the board room," Jace says.

A swell of nostalgia washes into the office, taking Jace on an epic ride along a wave called memory lane. I need to spend more time up here, taking in the little things. That first day in the store, I was so excited to find that picture of Colby and

Shark in the midst of surf injuries and beach parties on the wall. I want to go back to that moment, just to feel that way again.

"We've gotta fix this mess," Jace says, pulling me away from the memory. "Can you talk to the other guys about Logan's idea? We need to get this surf lessons thing up and going pretty quickly. We need some good publicity, and we desperately need to drive some business in here."

"I'll handle it," I assure him.

It's only a few hours after lunch, but that doesn't mean anything to Miles Garrett. When I asked him and Emily to tag along with Topher and me for the afternoon, I didn't bother to tell them about my hidden agenda – also known as 'get the Hooligans onboard with Logan's idea to make Drenaline Surf look good.' All I had to say was 'burritos' and 'hang out.'

Topher sits in my driver's seat, with Miles behind him and Emily behind me. Even though Emily and I were right here at the drive-in last night, it didn't stop her from wanting to come back today. She only orders a grape slush this time, though. Miles, on the other hand, orders four breakfast burritos (at three o'clock in the afternoon), and Topher orders a cheeseburger. This is why they can't stand living with Colby Taylor.

"So, I need some surfer feedback," I say, angling toward Topher so he and Miles can both see me. "We've been trying to come up with something that would bring in new business, make Drenaline Surf look good, and get our surfers involved without making you stand behind the cash register."

Miles groans. "I'm just ready to be back in the water," he says.

"Exactly," I agree, hoping I can lead him into this. "What do you think about giving surf lessons?" I ask.

Before they can answer, our food is delivered. This will

106

work to my advantage because they won't be talking. As soon as Topher pays and the car-hop disappears, I give them the pitch I've been working on all day.

"Think about it. You get out of the store, into the ocean, get to surf during business hours, and you get a commission off any lessons you give," I say. "And you can do it once a week or whatever works with your schedule. Nothing is set in stone."

Topher tilts his head like a confused puppy, but I know that far away look that's in his eyes. He's thinking about it. He's playing it out in his head. Right now, he's out there in those crystal blue waters of Crescent Cove.

"I'm in," he says, far too easily.

"That was much simpler than I expected," I admit to him.

He smiles a classic Topher Brooks kind of smile. "I was just thinking about what it was like when I was a kid. Just a grom, frothing to get out there and catch my first wave," he says, still smiling. "Sometimes, when I get in the water, I remember that first day with Shark, him telling me when to pop up. It was the *best* feeling. He'd want me to do this."

I glance over at Miles. He shrugs and says something that sounds like 'sure' but it's hard to tell when he's teeth-deep in a burrito. Topher starts telling us about the first time he surfed in Horn Island, down by the pier, years before it collapsed. It was the day of his first wipe out, and he laughs when he says that he told Shark he was never surfing again afterward.

He begins to say something else but stops when he feels a shadow looming over him. I duck my head down near my car's radio to see the person who just walked up to my car. I don't recognize him. Apparently, neither does Topher.

My boyfriend cracks the window, just barely. "Can we help you?" he asks.

"Are you Topher Brooks?" the guy asks. "The guy who surfs for Drenaline Surf?"

A tight pain settles in my back, right along my spine. It's a familiar tension, the kind I feel every time something goes down and I know it's going to bite us later. I hate that I can't enjoy a single moment without worrying about the repercussions of everything we do.

"Yeah, that's me," Topher says. "Do I know you?"

The guy shakes his head. He can't be much older than us, if at all. He looks like a typical beach bum in board shorts and a T-shirt. His hair is a bit of a mess, like maybe he was in the ocean himself earlier today.

"Nah, but I've seen you surf before. Would you sign something for me? I think you'll be famous someday, so I should grab the autograph now," the guy says.

Any concern Topher had before now has flown out the cracked window. He turns to me, asking if I have any of his promo pictures with me – because, you know, PR reps should carry those things in her personal belongings.

"Seriously? I'm out with my boyfriend, not playing your manager at some event. I left your promo pics at home, babe," I tell him.

I hand him a pen from my purse, and Miles folds a burrito wrapper into a pretty little square. He signs his own name before letting Topher do the same.

A group of people huddle around my car, asking Topher and Miles for autographs and pictures. One girl asks someone else if they're famous, and Emily sighs loudly because she hates surf groupies. She stays in with me after Miles and Topher get out of the car to fake being famous for a few minutes.

"This is what I hate about the surf world," Emily says, nodding out the window. "Miles wouldn't get a second glance from some of those girls if he weren't a surfer, and you know, sponsored by an actual company."

She doesn't seem worried about her relationship status,

though. I don't think Miles would dare try to date anyone else. Emily feeds him and cheers him on, the two most important things in Miles Garrett's book.

It's a curious thing, though, to watch Topher interact with these strangers. He has a charisma that I imagine Shark had. He's outgoing, the life of the party, but he's persuasive and intriguing. He makes you want to keep up with him, to know what he's doing. These girls may not be surf fans yet, but I bet they'll leave here searching for him on Twitter or Instagram.

"You know there's this stereotype, right?" Emily asks from the backseat. "Surfers date supermodels. Look at the world tour. Nearly every girlfriend on there is a model of some sort. Bikini models. You'll see guys like Miles dating girls like you wouldn't even believe."

I push away the remarks that Colby made before my weekend away with Topher. I refused to accept it, even if I possibly believed it, but he's right – Topher would be the one to get wrapped up in the whirlwind of being a famous surfer. He wants to be adored. He wants people to want to be his friend. When you're from a place like Horn Island and have the reputation of being rough around the edges, who doesn't want to overcome that and be a rock star? He may have Hooligan blood, and I truly believe when it's all said and done, he'll be back in Horn Island hanging with his friends, but Topher may be the one who wants to branch out and live the superstar life for a while. Move over, Colby Taylor.

"At least we're breaking the stereotype," Emily says. It seems like she says it more for herself than for me, but right now, I think I need to hear it as much as she does.

After dropping Emily and Miles off at Emily's car, Topher asks me to go back to the condo rather than taking him to Colby's house.

"Go change," he says, as soon as I park my car. "We're

going to the beach. No arguments."

I can't remember the last time I had a beach day. I think my last trip to the beach was the night Topher ended up in the hospital. For a moment, I hesitate changing into beach attire, but it's sort of like crashing a car or falling off a bike. The best way to overcome it is to just try again.

After putting on my bikini, I pull a pair of shorts and a Drenaline Surf T-shirt on over it. Topher lingers outside of the condo's guest house waiting for me.

"Which beach?" I ask. I drape two beach towels over my arm.

"Here," Topher says. "Behind your house."

As often as I trek through the sand and roam along the shoreline behind the house, I think the last time I really hung out back here on the beach was last summer. I sat on this very sand talking to Vin about coming back this summer. I said goodbye to Miles and Topher just off to my right. Kale programmed his number into my phone over there.

Last summer seems as if it happened in another lifetime, yet it's so close right now that I can almost feel it again. There was an energy floating over the water back then, a magical aura that you can't really put into words because no words are worthy.

Topher takes the beach towels and stretches them out on the sand. I take a seat next to him, watching the colors of the sky swish together. It's that time of the day when the sunset is lazy, so the colors aren't quite as bold. Soft pink and sherbet orange linger around drifts of pastel blues, weaving around each other like ballerinas of the sky, dancing to the sound of the waves rather than Tchaikovsky.

"What's the one thing you wish you had in your life right now that's missing?" Topher asks, like it's a normal, easy question.

Where do I even begin with that? I wish I had less drama,

more stability, an idea of what I was doing with my life, or just a day of peace where I don't have to wait for the other shoe to drop.

"I want that feeling back that I had last summer," I say, because it sums up everything I'm feeling. "That invincible feeling. That feeling that no matter what happens, there's something big ahead of me. Last summer was exciting and hopeful, and I couldn't wait to get back here and live it all out. But it's like ever since I came back, everything has been a one disaster after the next."

Topher nods but doesn't say anything. I hope he knows what I mean. I don't want to rewind and undo us. I don't want to take away his sponsorship or reverse to the easy days. I just want that forever-chasing feeling back. I want to feel like there's something more, something better, ahead of me. I want to know this is all worth it.

"I wish I could walk down to the shoreline and let the waves wash it all away, just carry all of the drama back out to sea," I say.

It'd be so easy to just leave it with the seahorses and mermaids, the sharks and shipwrecks. All of the tabloid articles and mug shots could just hang out in a treasure chest, so far away from land that no one would think of it ever again.

Topher jumps up from his towel and reaches a hand down for me.

"C'mon. Get up. You're coming with me," he says. He pulls his shirt over his head and tosses it onto the sand.

"Where are we going?" I ask. I grasp his hand and let him pull me to my feet.

"To wash it all away," he says.

I follow suit and leave my outer clothing on the beach towel. Topher tugs me closer to him and starts toward the water.

"I'll tell you like I always told my brother," he says. "The ocean isn't going to work for you if you stay on the shoreline. Besides, the last time I got you in the water with me, I was unconscious. I'd like to have at least one memory of us in the water that doesn't involve anyone drowning."

He wastes no time rushing into the oncoming waves, letting them throw him off balance. He falls back into the water, waves rushing over his skin and washing away any worries that he may have had two minutes ago.

"You can't think about it," he calls out, drifting further into the ocean. He pulls his arm back and slings water in my direction. "Get in!"

I shut off the part of my brain that feels silly and just go with it. This time, I'm not racing into the water to find him among the blackness of the night. I'm not fighting Mother Nature to let him live. There are no surfboards to hold on to or leashes to detach. No one has to call Theo or an ambulance. No one is trapped on crutches unable to help. No one cries on the shoreline.

It feels like summer, but here, it's always summer.

I return the favor and splash water back in Topher's general direction. He laughs but paddles toward me. His arms wrap around me, pulling me into him, letting us drift with the waves.

The looming sunset reflects on the water, glowing around us in hues of bright, bold colors. The water glistens, like a rainbow of stained glass floating on the surface.

Topher presses his forehead against mine. "This is why I surf," he says, his voice low. "There's nothing that makes the world better than the ocean…except this."

And he presses his lips to mine.

CHAPTER 17

Sleeping in on your day off isn't possible when you work for Drenaline Surf. My phone buzzes against the nightstand, but I refuse to open my eyes. I want to linger in yesterday's sunset just a little longer. I want to stay in the ocean, under the colors that remind me of seahorses and paper stars. I want to stay lost in the blues of Topher's eyes.

Buzzzzz.

Damn it. I push myself off of the mattress, open my eyes against my will, and grab my cell phone.

Eight new messages.

I open the most recent one, the one that forced me to face reality instead of live in yesterday's fantasy. Damn you, Alston Wright.

Are you ever going to wake up? Turn on SurfTube. Drama. All the drama.

There's no way I'm dragging myself over to the condo to watch the TV right now. Instead, I pull up my SurfTube app and start the stream from the beginning. At least I can watch our company go up in flames from the comfort of my own bed.

"Good morning, surf fans!" Bridget Parker says at the beginning of the broadcast. "The last few days have been crazy on the west coast, and today, I'm joined by Mr. Greg Carson of Liquid Spirit who's going to give us the dirty details of what went down at the recent event held in Crescent Cove."

I shake my head before he even comes on screen. Bridget Parker gets on my ever-last nerve, but she's quite possibly the face of SurfTube. Sometimes I think she'd be better in Hollywood, interviewing people on the red carpet and talking about who designed their clothing. Bridget herself is always dressed in designer heels with big hair and flawless makeup to match. I can't help but wonder how she manages on the sand in her stilettos.

The camera shifts to her sitting under a tent on the beach, microphone in hand. Greg Carson is on the chair next to her. She crosses her tanned legs, showing more skin than most of the surfers.

"Good morning, Greg, and thank you for joining us so bright and early today," she says.

"Thank you for having me," he replies. "There's no better way to start the day than visiting with SurfTube."

Oh, what BS. Does Greg Carson even know how stupid he looks right now? Bridget wears a too-short sundress with bright pink earrings to match. She looks summery. He, on the other hand, sits in a suit, tie, and dress shoes. I understand being a professional but c'mon, this is California and you work for a surf corporation. Suit and tie? Really?

"Some of your surfers were involved in a physical altercation last weekend prior to the start of the event," Bridget explains. "Could you tell us, in your own words, exactly what happened?"

I flip over onto my stomach and prop my phone against the headboard so I can actually watch this as if I were lying in bed watching TV. There's nothing he can say right now that I haven't already anticipated.

"And while I won't pretend my guys were innocent bystanders, I will be the first to say that Liquid Spirit believes in professionalism," Greg continues after explaining that Jace threw the first punch.

Sadly, everything he's said thus far is pretty much on target. You don't have to spread rumors or lies about the enemy when they really did lose control and make their company look badly.

"I've spoken to my boys about watching their mouths at events and keeping opinions to themselves," he states. "This is something we probably should have discussed before arriving at the event and maybe it would've prevented some of what happened, but at the end of the day, we aren't responsible for other people's actions or how they handle a situation. I'm just thankful that no one was seriously injured and that we were allowed to compete that day. Every event opens new doors for our surfers, and we want them to thrive in this community."

There's a piece of me that hates how well he's handling this. He says all of the right things. He takes his jabs without actually taking them. He's mastered the 'read between the lines' press statements. Greg Carson may be a snake in the grass who wants nothing more than for us to fail, but he's damn good at snaking.

Bridget tucks a loose hair behind her ear as the breeze drifts under the tent. "So there's no ill will or hard feelings?" she asks.

"You know, Bridget, I honestly don't blame Jace Hudson for what happened," Greg says, tilting his head and staring off at the sand as if in deep contemplation. "It's not his fault that he was thrown into a position that he wasn't ready for. Drenaline Surf was already coming apart at the seams before he stepped into that job, and he's just trying to put out the fires that were burning before he arrived."

I sit up on my bed and grab my phone. I don't trust this guy, and I don't trust where this conversation may be heading. After all that's happened, personal and professional, I'm not okay with anyone blaming Vin for Drenaline Surf's problems *or* for leaving. We've all just been doing the best we can to keep this store alive and to keep Shark's legacy growing.

Greg Carson shakes his head, opens his mouth to say something, and then pulls a 'never mind' afterward, leaving Bridget and viewers – and yeah, me – wondering what he was about to say.

"This is your moment," Bridget reminds him, as if he

were about to actually surf in a final and prove that he's worthy of being sponsored. "If you want our viewers and surf fans to know something, no time is better than the present."

Greg readjusts his tie, pretending to feel stressed over this, but in reality, he's just playing it up for the camera. That man is bursting to say whatever it is that he's preparing for.

"The real problem with Drenaline Surf has always been Shark McAllister," he explains.

Well, I didn't see that one coming. Vin, sure. Colby, of course. But Shark? Hell no.

"I don't want to speak ill of those no longer with us, but the man founded a company and built it around one surfer whose entire existence was a fraud," he says, taking the jab at Colby, as I expected. "When your business is built on lies, manipulation, and deception, you can't expect success to follow, no matter how talented the surfer is."

At least he gives credit where it's due. Colby has all the talent in the world, something Shark was more than aware of. Colby was an intermediate level surfer when he walked into Drenaline Surf for the first time. Shark McAllister made Colby who he is, in more ways than one.

"I can't help that Drenaline Surf was built on corruption and lies. I can't change the damage that's been done. I have no control over what they do within their business," Greg says. Then he points to the camera. "But I'm making it my personal mission to restore the love for this sport and to build our surf community back up to what it was years ago. You can mark my words."

After thanking Greg for his time and honesty, Bridget reminds everyone to drop by Liquid Spirit's new location and check out their soon-to-open wave pool in a few weeks. She closes the segment by offering well wishes and prayers to the shark attack victim in Sunrise Valley.

I scroll through my other texts – all from Alston, A.J., and one from Reed – and tell my roommates that I've seen the footage. A.J. says it's bullshit, and Alston thinks we should riot. Reed agrees with me that A.J. and Alston both need to chill and keep their mouths shut.

After I take a shower, which sadly didn't wash away any of the drama from this morning's SurfTube segment, I see a missed call on my phone. It's from Drenaline Surf.

Jace's voicemail asks me to come to the store. So much for a day off. It looks like I'm going to be fighting back to Greg Carson's interview after all. On the drive to the store, I play with phrases in my mind, just like Vin used to do, hoping to come up with the best wording. Hopefully Jace will get better at this in time and be able to structure a press statement to hold them over on my days off.

But something is wrong when I get to Drenaline Surf. It's closed. My heart thumps rapidly as I dig through my purse to find my store keys. I can barely grasp them long enough to unlock the door because my hands won't stop shaking. There's absolutely no reason the store should be closed – unless someone died, and I refuse to even go there.

Emily stands in front of the counter, opposite from her usual place on the other side. Kale leans against it, elbows resting on the edge. The light is off in the surfboard room, and only the fluorescent light above the cash register is on in here. It's eerily quiet. My keys sound like an out of tune instrument when I drop them back into my purse.

The noise is enough to drag Jace into the room. He doesn't look professional today. He stands before us in ripped jeans and a faded black band tee. I'm not familiar with Frozen Bloodstream, I don't like the fact that he's wearing this shirt right now. Drenaline Surf's bloodstream seems to be frozen at the moment.

"I'm sorry to make you guys come up here, but I needed to speak with each of you individually," he says. "Kale, you want to come back with me first?"

Kale hesitates. "Is something wrong? Like, do I need to bring Haley with me or something?" he asks. "She manages my career, so if something's wrong, maybe she needs to hear it too."

Jace looks at the floor, away from us, and then finally turns his attention back to his Hooligan brother. "That's up to you," he says. "But you may prefer to do this on your own, given this situation."

What the hell is that supposed to mean? I'm more than capable of handling this job. I make Colby Taylor look good, and that is something no one has been able to do since Shark McAllister.

"Anything you have to say to me, you can say in front of Haley and Emily," Kale informs him. "So go ahead."

The tired expression on Jace's face worries me. He clearly doesn't want to have this conversation, at least not with all of us at once, but he throws his hands into the air and mumbles something about how he warned us.

He positions himself on the other side of the counter, next to the cash register. I squeeze in between Emily and Kale.

"There is no easy way to say this," Jace begins. "You're all well aware of the rumors, the legal issues, and everything else that's been happening to Drenaline Surf lately. But something has come up that's a bit more serious than Colby's parents or A.J.'s juvenile record. It's even bigger than my arrest."

My guts feel like the sign at Shipwrecked, tangled up in the tentacles of a massive octopus. It squeezes and twists, leaving me nauseated.

"I can't go into the details, but this turn of events is something that requires extreme measures while it's being investigated," he explains. "I didn't want to make this decision, but it's for the good of Drenaline Surf, and that's what I have to take into consideration. So until further notice, the three of you are being placed on administrative leave."

CHAPTER 18

I'm livid. I'm bullet-spitting kind of livid. And I'm upset because I don't understand how I can go from putting out Drenaline Surf fires to possibly *being* a Drenaline Surf fire. But more than anything, I'm scared.

Emily doesn't say a word as she leans against her driver's side door. She hasn't said a word this entire time. She just fiddles with the small sea turtle keychain that she kept her work keys on, holding it all on its lonesome.

Even when Vin fired me, he didn't take my keys from me. I've had those keys since the day Vin met my parents, when he gave me the set in case I ever needed to find him and couldn't. Now, I'm Drenaline Surf-less.

"I wonder how long we can stand here before he sends someone to escort us away," Emily says, looking at her rhinestone-encrusted flip-flops. "Banned from the premises. How did this even happen?"

What is possibly bigger than criminal records? What could they be hiding that's worth suspending your PR rep and putting a sponsorship on hold?

"I need this job. Nowhere else is going to pay me this well without some fancy college degree. I have no reason to hurt Drenaline Surf," Emily says. Her voice cracks and she grabs her sunglasses from her purse. "I'm leaving before he calls his friend Pittman to see me off. I'll call you later."

She doesn't give me a chance to console her or even say goodbye. I'm surprised she managed to stay an extra five minutes in the parking lot with me. She fought tears from the very moment that Jace asked for her keys.

I watch the back door until Kale emerges. For half a second, I'm hopeful that maybe the Hooligan brotherhood worked in Kale's favor, but he shakes his head as he walks my way.

"Do you believe this? I really thought if I talked to him one-on-one, maybe he'd tell me something, but he's in serious boss-mode," Kale tells me.

"Nothing at all?" I ask.

"Pretty much, no," Kale confirms. "He said that when we're eligible to work for Drenaline Surf again – *if* we're eligible – we'll be notified by Joe or whoever is in charge at that time."

"If we're eligible? He actually said that?" I question. That's a huge freaking if. "How did we even get here? And what does he mean whoever is in charge? You think his job is on the line too?"

Kale shrugs. "I'm as lost as you are. This is bullshit," he says. "Was this the master plan? Take us down one by one? I can't believe I could lose my sponsorship over this. We all just basically lost our jobs."

If the plan was to take us down one by one, whoever is behind this started with Kale, Emily, and me. Maybe they thought we were the easiest to eliminate. We're the weakest links…or the easiest targets.

But then it dawns on me. We're under investigation. Jace or Joe or maybe both of them have a reason to believe it's one of us. Something points in our directions. We're suspects. We're no longer innocent in the eyes of Drenaline Surf. If they have reason to doubt us, who else will believe we're guilty?

Kale says he's going to talk to the Hooligans about this and promises to update me if he hears anything else. I tell him the same before I get in my car and head back to the condo. I don't want to go home, though. How do I tell my roommates about this? What do I even say?

On the short drive, this all becomes sickeningly real to me. It's going to hit the tabloids tomorrow or the next day – whenever the story catches on and the gossip spreads.

SurfTube is going to discuss it. Surf forums online will talk about it. Residents of Horn Island and Crescent Cove will question us. And I have no way to defend myself. I can't even word the press statement, and for once, I don't trust Jace to do the job correctly.

A.J. walks outside as soon as I pull into the driveway. "I thought you were off today," he says. "What's up?"

I'm only one leg out of the car as he asks the questions.

"Why weren't you at work today?" I ask him. "Or Alston. Were you guys scheduled to be off?"

He shakes his head. "Jace called me this morning and said to take the day off per Joe, so I didn't question it. I needed the sleep," he says. "Are you okay?"

"No," I say, walking toward the guest house. Luckily, I know A.J. well enough to know he'll follow me inside. I don't want to have this conversation out in the open.

He sits on my bed and waits quietly as I tell him what happened today, from the store being closed to the moment I left after realizing Jace wasn't going to budge even for Kale.

When A.J. finally speaks, he says something I don't expect. "You know I'm behind you, right? No matter what happens, you have me."

I mean, yeah, I know that A.J. has my back. He's the only person in Crescent Cove who hasn't let me down in one way or another. Even when he threw me off the jet ski, that was a blessing in disguise because I realized how misunderstood he is.

"You don't think people will turn against me, do you?" I ask. I feel stupid even saying the words. There's no way we're going to fall apart over this.

He shrugs. "I'm just saying, if people start talking, you don't know what will happen," he says, scaring me more than I'd like. "Kale is a Hooligan. Emily dates one."

"So do I," I remind him. I grab my phone from my purse

and dial Topher's number, just to prove that he'll be there for me and has my back too.

But Topher doesn't answer. He's probably with Kale, getting the scoop on what happened. Or he's with Miles and Emily, helping his best friend console a crying girl. He'll call me back.

"How well do you know Emily?" A.J. asks, stretching out on my bed.

I can't believe he's even going there. Emily isn't guilty of this. She'd never hurt Drenaline Surf. Vin took a chance on her and gave her that job, and she's enjoyed every second of being part of this. And she adores her boyfriend. There's no way she'd ever hurt his sponsor.

"Don't do that," I tell A.J. "Don't start questioning everyone. Don't make me start questioning everyone."

"Sit down," he says, motioning to the bed. "I love you. You know that. You're my family. But I've been here. I've lived through this before. When Shark died, we all split. The Hooligans all came together, and the rest of us were on the outside. Vin was the only link between us, and he was with us more than them. I've seen it play out before. I want you to be prepared."

I don't understand why it has to be one of us. What happened to the Dominic theory? It's still very likely that he's pumping information to someone. What about Colby's parents? They may have an entire team of people working for them to drag Drenaline Surf down. They have the money. They're probably not as broke as they're pretending to be. If people think it's Kale, they could go after any of the Hooligans. It's only a matter of time before they say it's Miles or Theo. If people think it's me, it could just as easily be Alston or Logan. No one is safe.

"They're trying to take us down from the inside," I say, letting it all sink in against my will. "This was the plan. Turn us all against each other, right?"

A.J. shrugs. "I don't know what the plan is," he admits. "But I just know how easily people take sides around here. Shark's death, in some ways, tore us apart and in other ways, brought us together. But this is different. I just want you to be prepared. And no matter what, I'm on your side. I know you didn't do this. But I'll be honest – I can't say the same for Kale or Emily, and that's how I know someone will say the same about you."

After A.J. says to let him handle telling Reed and Alston, the panic sets in full force. If he doesn't want me to tell our own roommates, something is wrong. Maybe he knows how they'll react. Kale has become a good friend of Alston's, and Reed likes to stay neutral. It may just be me and Jailbird Gonzalez in the end, and while I love A.J., I don't want to lose everyone else along the way.

Once I know A.J. is inside and out of view, I grab my bag and make a run for the car. There's one other person in the cove who I know will have my back until the very end.

CHAPTER 19

"You can't let this get to you," Colby says for the tenth time. He resituates in the corner of his couch. "Everyone knows you have Drenaline Surf's best interests at heart. You always have."

I don't say a word, but I narrow my eyes at him, hoping he gets the message. The more I think about it, the more guilty I can see myself being, even though I know better. I'm not from here. I'm friends with Colby. I'm only here because of him. His parents arrived in the cove the very same day I did.

Kale was right – I've read so many gossip articles and theories that I can actually predict them now. I can think like the columnists, even when I'm the one being talked about.

"Everything is stacked against me," I tell Colby. "I dated Vin, and he bailed. Then I dated his brother. I look like I'm dating around within the Drenaline Surf family so I can gather info or keep my in with them."

He laughs, and I'm borderline offended because I'm being so incredibly serious right now. I know it sounds ridiculous. I hear the words as they come out of my mouth. I realize I'm reaching the crazy point, but it doesn't matter.

"I need to be a step ahead so I can brace myself for the storm," I say.

"Then become a weatherman. Or weather-woman. Or whatever," Colby says. "Think about it. Emily is dating her high school best friend's ex-boyfriend. That looks shady. Kale isn't even from here, and people could say he was bitter about the honorary Hooligan status or that he wants to go back to Hawaii."

I don't like his theories. I don't like the idea that Emily or Kale is dishonest. I know better. My heart knows better. But he has a point. Emily isn't as well-known in the Drenaline Surf world, so all kinds of dirt could be dug up on her. She's a blank slate for the most part, as far as the media is concerned. And Kale isn't from here, so they could easily paint some shady past and evil motives around him. We really were the easiest targets.

"Or hey, Vin is behind it all and that's why he bailed," Colby suggests. "He's not on an oil rig. He's in hiding. Do you see how stupid this is? I can spin it any way I want. Hell, maybe it's me and I'm working with my parents and this was all part of the plan. Make me a famous surfer. Have a crazy story for the media. My parents fake a lawsuit, and we all get rich and famous in the process. See what I mean?"

"Point taken," I say, defeated. Who knew I'd need Colby Taylor to talk sense into me someday?

"You want to go for a ride?" he asks. "Just to get some air and clear your head?"

Right now, nowhere sounds better than his pier. After today, I don't think I trust the ocean to wash away the drama and worries of my world. If anything, I feel like she's taunting me, daring me to test her again. Next time, she may not be as generous as she was the night she released Topher for us. Solid land is where I belong right now.

"He's still not answering," I say, slamming my phone into the cup holder in Colby's truck.

After multiple calls and text messages, I thought I'd have heard something from Topher by now. Emily hasn't responded to my text either, but I haven't blown up her phone like I have with Topher's. I just wanted to know if she was okay. I'm a little offended that Topher hasn't bothered to do the same for me. He has to know by now. Kale is a Hooligan, and Miles is his best friend. Of course, he knows by now.

"Do you think he thinks I'm guilty?" I ask, even thought I don't want to know the answer.

Colby shrugs, which is what I feared. He was here when Shark died. He watched the same thing that A.J. watched. He saw them come together and push everyone else away. Is that what's happening now? Am I being ditched by a Brooks brother yet again? I really don't like this pattern.

Colby pulls his truck into a parking lot near the outskirts of Crescent Cove. There's a boating ramp off to the side. A red and white sign catches Colby's headlights. It has stick figure drawings explaining how to properly launch and dock from out here.

I've only driven out this far once, and I was with Vin. But even that one time was enough to be familiar with the area. Shark's studio is out here somewhere, all alone, away from the crowd.

I wonder if Shark used to drive out there whenever the surf world got to be too much. I bet it was his Zen place the way the pier is for Colby. I spin around in my seat to look out the back glass.

Dusk is upon us, in that hazy way where orange streaks turn gray in the sky, but it's fitting for today. There is no beautiful sunset with bright colors hiding behind palm tree leaves. It's not camera-worthy, even though I know that Shark could've captured it with his lens in a way to make it beautiful.

"Is that it?" I ask, pointing back behind us.

Colby laughs. "Is it crazy that I know exactly what 'that' is without you telling me?" he asks. "Yeah, that's Shark's studio back there. I haven't been in it since he died."

I squint my eyes to see it in the haze, but I know it's over there with that oval-shaped sign above the front door. *Jake McAllister Photography.* It's the same silver logo that's on all of his photographs.

"Okay, I know it's been a long day," I begin, "and I know you think I'm crazy, but...is there a light on in his studio?

Please tell me I just can't see correctly and the craziness has gone to my eyesight."

Colby whips his truck around in the empty boating lot and throws it back into PARKED. He pops his door open and peers into the distance. "Looks like it," he says.

"There's no way," I insist, opening my own door. "Kill your headlights."

Colby does as he's ordered. The creeping nightfall proves him right, though. There's a light on in Shark's studio, which is impossible.

"Oh God," I say, steadying my balance against his truck door. My head swims with panic, and I fear I may hit the pavement.

"Get in," Colby says, getting back into the driver's seat.

He reaches his hand across to help me back into the truck. I feel so incredibly fragile.

"Maybe it's Joe or one of the guys," Colby says. "We'll drive over and see if anyone's car is there, okay?"

I nod quickly, but I can't calm the leaps my heart is trying to take across my chest cavity. My lungs feel heavy, but I'm thankful for their positioning or else my heart may have seriously already leapt out of my chest. I feel like a dolphin out of water.

"Are you okay?" Colby asks. "Take a deep breath."

I shake my head. "There are only two people with keys to that studio," I tell him. "Joe doesn't have one. And the Hooligans don't have access. There was only one spare key."

Digging through my purse, I unzip the side pocket where I've had the key stashed since Vin gave it to me a few weeks ago. Then I hold it up to show Colby.

"You have the spare?" he asks, a bit surprised.

I nod. "And the other key is on an oil rig."

As Colby turns onto the street that leads down to the studio, I try to convince myself that maybe Vin gave the key back to Joe. He turned Drenaline Surf over to him, so maybe he turned over the studio too. But then Joe would've gotten my key from me or Vin would've asked for it back. Someone would've said something, regardless.

The thought of someone digging around through Shark's belongings, touching his photography equipment and leaving prints on his photos, makes me absolutely sick. I don't even come out here, and I'm technically allowed to. This is like hallowed ground. It's sacred. Knowing someone has been here – or is in there right now – is worse than being placed on administrative leave. I was trusted with this place, and I haven't even kept a proper eye on it. Now someone is using it to probably gain more information, to find new secrets or ways to bring us down. Maybe whatever 'turn of events' that happened today has to do with this. Why didn't I come out here sooner?

A white car is parked outside of the studio. I don't recognize it. Neither does Colby.

"Arkansas tags," Colby says. "Why is someone from a land-locked state at Shark's studio?"

I rush through my mind trying to remember if we stopped anywhere in Arkansas last summer on our scavenger hunt across America. I don't recall it, though. Stella's was in Tennessee. The coffee shop was in Oklahoma. Did we even go through Arkansas?

"Let's go in," I tell him. "I'm not running from them."

"Should we call someone? Let them know?" Colby asks.

I glance over at him as I pop the door open. "Who are you going to call? Joe? Jace? Pittman? You can call if you want, but I'm going in," I say.

I slam the truck door behind me, just so whoever is inside will know I'm here and I'm coming in with a vengeance. Colby eases up behind me, sans phone.

"If we die in a few minutes, thank you for believing in

me," he says.

For the first time today, I actually smile. "You have nine lives, Taylor," I remind him. "If anyone lives through this, it'll be you."

My key proves itself pointless when we walk around the sidewalk to the front entrance. The door is already cracked open, so I waste no time and push it forward. A metal file cabinet slams shut, and he turns around to face me.

"Haley Elise Sullivan," he says, shaking his head. "I should've known you'd be the one to find me."

It hits me harder than Jace hit the Liquid Spirit jerk. It's that feeling – that last summer, forever-chasing, there's hope for the world after all feeling.

From the depths of my brain, I pull out the vocals from an old memory. It's Reed's voice, announcing the 'man of the hour.'

And now here he stands, in Shark's photography studio, staring back at me with those blue eyes that haunt me even now – Vin Brooks.

CHAPTER 20

"Well, this is awkward," Colby says, shoving his hands into the pockets of his cargo shorts. "I think I'll wait outside. You know, to keep watch or something."

I think he's officially made this more awkward than it would have been if he'd just kept his mouth shut. He pulls the door closed behind him on his exit, leaving me standing in Shark's studio facing my ex-boyfriend who isn't even supposed to be on the west coast.

I open my mouth, but my vocal chords grab onto the words and hold them tightly, refusing to let them exit my mouth. I have so many questions. But I can't ask them.

"I was searching for a spare set of keys to Drenaline Surf," Vin says, like it's not a big deal that he's here…in California…in his best friend's photography studio…with me.

"Who knows you're here?" I ask. I can't budge from this spot near the door. I feel like I should stay here, though, just in case I need to run.

"Joe's the only one," Vin says, glancing away from me. He opens the next drawer on the file cabinet and searches through it. "Well, now you and Taylor know, obviously."

He keeps his back to me as he pulls USB cords out of the cabinet. I doubt Shark hid extra keys in there, but I don't tell him that. He crams the items back in and slams the drawer shut.

"I know I owe you a lot of answers," he finally says, bracing himself against the cabinet. "But it's not safe to talk here. Can we go somewhere else?"

Go somewhere and talk? Has he completely forgotten the last few weeks?

"You can't just show up here like nothing happened," I say.

I try to choke back all of the emotions that I want to throw at him, but they're begging to be let out of the glass jar I've been keeping them locked away in. I don't know which feeling wants to riot first, but based upon the sudden rage I feel upon seeing him, I think anger is leading the way.

"Haley, I know I fucked up a lot of things, and I know I let a lot of people down, but I can explain things," he says, keeping his voice calm. I wonder if he's even nervous.

"Why are you here?" I ask. He has to know what's going on. There's no other reason for him to randomly show up in Crescent Cove again.

"Can we please go back to Taylor's house and talk there?" Vin asks, easing across the room closer to me. He stops a few feet away. "We really don't need to be here."

As much as I want to hear what he has to say, I don't trust him right now. Hell, I don't know if I trust anyone other than A.J. and Colby. For all I know, Vin knows everything and he's here to bring me down just like Liquid Spirit and Dominic and whoever the hell else is behind this.

"Does Topher know you're here?" I ask, ignoring his request to leave Shark's studio.

I hate being rude and harsh in front of the gorgeous photographs lining the walls. Shark's masterpieces shouldn't have to witness this awkward and angry reunion. I should've sent them out the door with Colby. At least they'd be in a safer place instead of hanging around while I blast Vin with questions.

When Vin doesn't answer, I realize that he hasn't even told his own brother about his return. I don't care what kind of bad blood exists between them now. Topher deserves to know that his brother is back in the cove. I grab my phone from my pocket, but Vin knows my move before I even hit Topher's name to dial.

"Don't call him," Vin says. "He won't answer for you."

I ignore his warning and press the call button. Then I send up a prayer that Topher *does* answer this time so I don't look like the ultimate idiot. When my call is immediately rejected and sent to voicemail, I want to cry, but I'll be damned before I let Vin see me cry over this.

Vin doesn't show an ounce of emotion as I put my phone back into my pocket. Instead, he holds up his own phone, selects Topher's name, and calls him. He puts the call on speaker phone. Topher answers after two rings.

"Hey kid," Vin says. "What are you doing?"

"Hanging out with Miles," Topher's voice says through the speaker.

"Everything okay?" Vin asks. "Joe called me earlier, and I just wanted to check on you."

"I'm good," Topher tells him. "I'm over at Kale's. Emily and Miles are here too. We're going to stay here tonight. Kale needs us, and Emily's been upset."

Vin glances my way, but I can't even break down. I can't feel much of anything at this point. What am I supposed to feel? Hurt? Betrayed? Broken? I don't think I have the energy to feel anything other than defeated.

"Okay, well, just take care of yourself, okay?" Vin says. "And call me if you need anything."

Topher says he will, and the call ends after a quick goodbye. So that's how it is now. Topher is avoiding me. We're right back there, back where we were after the kiss-and-run incident. He wasn't kidding. Running away from things is the one thing he is definitely good at doing.

"Just so you know, I didn't want to have to do that," Vin says. His voice is sincere, which I hate even more right now than ever before. "I'll answer your questions if you'll let me follow you to Colby's house."

I don't bother giving him an answer because I know him well enough to know he'll follow me out of plain stubbornness.

"This is fucking weird as hell," Colby says as we pull into his driveway. Vin's rental car pulls in behind us. "Are you not freaking out?"

Of course I'm freaking out. I lost my job – again – today, and this time it wasn't because I interfered with Vin's plans for his little brother. This is because someone wants to frame me or my friends for bringing Drenaline Surf down from the inside.

We enter through the garage, which is weird because I've always gone into Colby's house through the back door. He and Vin avoid eye contact with each other as we settle into Colby's living room.

"Start talking," I say immediately, not giving Vin a chance for small talk or stupid questions. I want answers, and I want them now. I point to the couch and am actually surprised when Vin sits without argument.

"Joe called me earlier this week," he starts, without any hesitation. "He'd been sending me links to the online articles and forum threads, so I've been keeping up from a distance."

Colby doesn't bother to sit. Instead, he leans over the back of a chair, propping his arms against the top of it. It's almost like he doesn't want to be in the same oxygen bubble as Vin. I wish their tension and dislike didn't run so deeply. I sit on the other end of the couch, closer to Colby than my ex.

"I don't know what went down today, but Drenaline Surf is being blackmailed, and apparently it's really bad," Vin says. "Joe wouldn't even tell me what the blackmail is, but it's something he definitely doesn't want going public."

"Well, if you're looking for an answer, I don't have it," I tell him.

"I know you don't," Vin says. "When Joe found out from Jace about the blackmail, he called me and asked if I could fly back home. Jace gave his resignation today, shortly after he talked to you, Emily, and Kale. He said he couldn't stay any longer."

"Jace resigned?" Colby asks. "So who's running Drenaline Surf now?"

"Well, technically, it's always been mine," Vin admits, shrugging like it's not a huge deal. "Joe never put it back in his name, and he said if I want Drenaline Surf back, I can have it, so here I am."

Wait a minute. My brain races to catch up with everything. Jace is gone. Vin is back. Vin actually *wants* Drenaline Surf, and did he say he knows I'm innocent?

I lean forward, halfway across the couch. "Say that again," I tell him.

"I'm back?" he asks.

"No, the other part. You know I'm not blackmailing Drenaline Surf," I say.

I need to hear him say it. I need someone other than my roommate with a criminal record and my best friend with a lawsuit to believe in me. I need someone credible. I need someone to take my side who probably shouldn't be on my side.

"You're not blackmailing Drenaline Surf," Vin says, putting the words into the universe. "When Joe told me about it, I ruled you out immediately. I know you. You'd never do this."

It's the most bizarre feeling. It's like I'm back on the sand while A.J. drinks Milwaukee Best and Vin talks about Logan and the future of Drenaline Surf. There's truth and belief and a future. There's something magical in the atmosphere, even though we were broken down on the side of the road that night. It's magical right now, here in Colby's living room, with Shark's photography on the walls. There's truth and belief, and I may actually have a future still.

Colby walks around the chair and motions for me to move down so he can sit. I don't hesitate. I scoot closer to Vin, letting Colby have the corner.

"Alright, Brooks," Colby says. "Let's have it. What do you know? What can we do?"

Vin explains that the most recent blackmail is related to a phone conversation that happened the night of the inventory crisis. It was after Logan left, leaving only Emily, Kale, and me in the store to possibly hear something.

"I don't know what they talked about, but it was between Jace and Joe," Vin says. He runs a hand through his hair, seemingly frustrated to be on the outside of this. "Whatever they talked about is at risk of being leaked, and they'll shut down Drenaline Surf before they let it get out."

If I hadn't been scared before, I'm scared now. That's why the store was closed today. I wonder if the blackmailers demanded that Drenaline Surf shut down or go out of business. Are they demanding money? Is there a payoff or do they want us to be a puppet, playing into their game while they pull all of the strings? And who the hell is this person or people?

Vin looks past me at Colby. "Do you remember Jake's memorial service? The one at the actual funeral home before the paddle out?" he asks.

I glance over at Colby. He nods and then looks at his carpet, like he doesn't want to go back there. I didn't know there was a memorial service outside of the paddle out. Maybe I need to just trap these two in Colby's house, force them to make peace, and then tell me everything because I'm sick of being on the outside.

"Remember how everyone split apart? How Topher refused to even speak to Reed and Miles told A.J. to fuck off?" Vin asks. "We're entering that again. Lines are drawn. People are choosing sides."

That's it. Crescent Cove versus Horn Island. My roommates versus the West Coast Hooligans. That was made perfectly clear tonight when Vin called Topher. He chose his Hooligans over me, without so much as giving me a chance to explain my side of the story. And Emily is with them by default, because she and Miles have been together much longer than I've been with Topher.

"So that's how it goes down," I say, sinking into the couch cushions. "They join forces, and I'm the girl from North Carolina who clearly can't be trusted. It's like I can feel California slipping through my fingers."

Colby sighs. "I'm sorry," he says. "You just happened to make friends with two of Crescent Cove's worst. But on the bright side, you still have A.J. and me."

"And your job," Vin adds. "Jace is gone. No one else is doing PR for me. It's either you or no one. And for what it's worth, I'm here."

He's here? But for how long? As soon as the smoke settles, he'll be gone again. He's here to clean up the mess that is Drenaline Surf. When it's fixed, he'll take a paycheck for his hard work, hand Joe the keys, and walk away again, just as a hero instead of the villain. This is his chance at redemption. And I don't know if I can even trust him.

"You're lying," I say. "You won't turn against your own brother. I don't care what happens. You'll side with Topher in the end because that's what you do. You have Horn Island in your veins. In the end, you'll join Team Kale and Emily Are Innocent."

Vin leans in toward me, staring me down like the day I met him on The Strip.

"Haley, do you think I'd be in Colby Taylor's living room if I didn't believe in you? You can deny it, but you know me well enough to know that I'm biting the hell out of my tongue to play nice with him right now for you," he says. "You can tell me every bad thing you think about me when this is over, but for now, I need you to let me be on your side, so are you gonna let me in or not?"

CHAPTER 21

I feel like I'm in the witness protection program sitting outside of the precinct this morning. It's a few minutes after eight o'clock when Vin finally takes off his sunglasses and asks if I'm ready.

"You sure you don't want me to go with you?" he asks. "I don't care if people find out I'm back. I just don't want Pittman taking advantage of this."

"He won't," I say. I never thought I'd be defending Officer Pittman, but I know that he won't abuse this moment. "I don't want people to see us together. We can't afford more rumors, and you can't blow your cover. People can't know you're on my side, right?"

Vin lets out a defeated sigh. He lets the seat back in his rental car and puts his sunglasses back on.

"You win," he says. "I'll lay low, but if you're not back in fifteen minutes, I'm coming in for you."

I skim the parking lot to make sure no one is around before getting out of the white car with the Arkansas plates. I remove my sunglasses at the door and take a deep breath before going inside. This is my only shot. I can't blow it.

"Can I help you?" the deputy behind the counter asks.

"I need to see Alex Pittman," I tell him, trying to keep a friendly tone in my nervous voice.

He rings into another office and tells Pittman that a young lady is here to see him. Fortunately, Pittman emerges instantly, probably expecting his girlfriend or someone instead of me.

"Haley?" he asks. "Is everything okay?"

I quickly nod and ask if I can speak with him in private. He leads me back to the office where he and Jace were the other day. He closes the door behind us, tells me to have a seat, and sits opposite of me at his desk.

"What brings you up here?" he asks.

"I need to hire a private investigator," I tell him. This may be a long shot, but I don't know where else to go. "I need a recommendation or referral. I figure you guys probably work with a few of them, and you could hook me up with the best."

He stares at me for a moment, not saying a word, studying me like he's unsure if I'm being honest. His eyes are dark but familiar, and part of me wants to know who he is – like who he *really* is when he's not some asshole cop arresting my best friend. Until recently, I'd never seen him as human.

"Is this about Drenaline Surf?" he asks.

I shrug. "Somewhat," I tell him. "It's also about Colby Taylor. I think his family is paying someone to find out anything they can about Drenaline Surf. It's become personal, so I want to take action."

Who knew the truth could be so easy? I played out a million different stories in my head this morning, trying to find something that sounded legal and safe yet still believable. I wasn't planning on being honest with Pittman, but the truth sounds better than any story I could've dreamed up.

"Look, you don't need a P.I.," he tells me. He glances at the door, like he's afraid someone may come inside. He brings his chair forward and props his elbows on the desk.

His voice is low when he speaks again. "If you need someone to check bank accounts, you need a computer hacker, not a private investigator," he says. "All they'll do is follow his parents around, maybe check phone records, and charge you by inflated hours."

Did a police officer just tell me I needed an illegal hacker to do this job for me? No wonder Vin wanted to come inside. This is exactly what he was talking about.

"With all due respect, Officer, I'm afraid that would be illegal," I tell him, crossing my leg over the other and retaining a straight posture. I won't be tricked. Just when I was beginning to think he had a soul…

"I didn't mean…I'm sorry. That came out wrong," Pittman says. "Look, I have a…contact…who owes me a favor. I can't exactly call him while I'm on the clock, but I'll give you my favor."

What a freaking set up. He's baiting me. If I was a preschooler, he'd hand me a lollipop and tell me that he's lost his puppy and needs help finding it. I can't believe he really thinks I'd fall for this.

"I'm sorry, but I'd prefer not to have a mug shot," I say. "Thank you for your time."

I stand quickly and hurry out of his office. Vin was right. I should have brought him in with me. Pittman wouldn't have pulled a stunt like that if he'd had iceberg eyes staring at him. I may run with criminals, but I'm not aiming to be one.

"What happened?" Vin asks, raising the driver's seat back up.

"We have to leave," I say, slamming the door behind me. "Now. Drive. Seriously. He tried to get me to hire an illegal computer hacker. He even offered to set it up for me."

Vin throws his sunglasses against the dashboard. "I'm talking to him," he says. "He's not going to set you up like that. I'm going inside."

Fuck. I do not need him going inside, making his presence known, and I definitely don't need him defending my honor. This isn't the time or place. Forget redemption, Vin. We have to leave.

But he gets out of the rental car and heads across the parking lot like a man on a mission.

And there's only one thing I can do – follow him inside.

"Alex Pittman, please," he says to the guy up front. "You can tell him Vin Brooks is here to see him."

Moments later, I'm back in the same chair, but this time,

an angry Vin Brooks is next to me.

"What the hell, Alex? Are you seriously trying to walk Haley into a trap?" he asks. "I really thought maybe you were in this job for the right reasons, but after the shit you've done to A.J. and now this? I should have them pull your badge."

Pittman takes the cursing like a pro. He sits silently, letting Vin say what he needs to say. The calmness actually disturbs me. I know it's probably part of his police training, to remain calm while a criminal or suspect is lashing out, but he's emotionless, sort of like how A.J. gets after an outburst. It's like the calm after the storm rather than before. I never thought I'd see them have something in common, aside from the same first initial.

"Are you done?" Pittman asks once Vin stops ranting and sits next to me.

"For now," Vin says. "What the fuck are you doing?"

"Helping you," Pittman says. "At least, I was trying to. I know I've done a lot of shit I shouldn't have, and I've abused my authority a time or two. I'm not going to pretend I'm perfect. I've screwed your friend over a few times before, so I thought if I helped you out, maybe it'd help make amends."

Does he really expect me to buy into that? He's screwed A.J. over by arresting him for no reason multiple times, so he's going to set me up with illegal activity to make peace? This guy is crazier than my screwed up friends – and Miles Garrett is pretty crazy.

"I can't do this here," Pittman says. "But if you come to my apartment tonight, when I'm off duty, I can help you out. Just me. Not Officer Pittman. Just Alex."

If I hadn't already thought that Vin was losing his mind, I'd think it now. We walk up a third flight of stairs because Pittman's apartment complex doesn't have an elevator.

"Thirty-one, oh-six," Vin says, reading the numbers off

the door. He knocks three times, and I hate this.

A deadbolt turns on the other side, and Pittman opens the door. He's in a pair of red flannel pajama pants and a white muscle shirt. I've never seen him in civilian clothing.

"I was starting to think you wouldn't show," he says. "C'mon in."

His living room is pretty bare. There's a futon in the middle of the room and a TV on a small stand. A stack of DVDs sits on the floor, and an X-Box is hooked up next to it.

A photo of him with an older man, probably his dad, rests on the ledge of the kitchen counter, facing into the living room. I invite myself over to look at it. A CD case for a Sebastian's Shadow album sits next to it, along with a set of keys and a bottle of Dasani water.

"So, tell me," Vin says, pacing the living room. "How does one of Crescent Cove's finest end up with a link to a computer hacker?"

Pittman offers us a seat, so I take one on the futon. Vin remains standing, though. Pittman leans against the kitchen counter, next to the picture of him and the older man.

"It was my first night on patrol," he says. "They had me doing random traffic stops, all the rookie shit that no one else wants to do. I was supposed to stop every sixth vehicle, and one was an eighteen-wheeler."

He moves from resting against the counter ledge and sits on the other end of the futon. He seems uncomfortable.

"The guy was just a kid, probably eighteen or nineteen. I asked him to put out his cigarette and told him I needed to see inside the back of the trailer," he explains.

He talks about the veteran cops who provided no back up or supervision for him. According to Pittman, they didn't expect him to last long outside of the academy. They thought he was a pretty boy who couldn't handle the heat.

"I was being set up to fail, and my dad had just been

diagnosed, so I was feeling like shit about my life at the time," he tells us.

I wish I hadn't come here tonight. I like the idea of him being an asshole cop. I don't want to see him as a human because he's spent years refusing to see A.J. as a human. He doesn't deserve any respect or sympathy.

"When the guy opened the truck, he had a... You're not going to believe me," he says, defeat evident in his voice.

"Try me," Vin says, walking over and standing in front of the futon.

"He had a dead toucan in the back," Pittman says, as clear as the cove's blue waters. "He was supposed to be disposing of it, legally, but he was keeping it to have his taxidermist friend stuff it. Everything about it was illegal and insane."

I don't want to believe this insanity – because that's exactly what it is – but I don't think Alex Pittman is creative enough to come up with something like this had it not actually happened. Even if he could weave a wild story, I don't think he'd share it with Vin or me.

"Did you take him in?" I ask.

He shakes his head. "The guy told me about a friend of his who was dying of leukemia. He was just a little older than me, and he couldn't leave his house because he was so sick. He couldn't go on adventures, so they were bringing the adventures to him," Pittman says.

He shrugs, like it's not that big of a deal, but it's still the weirdest thing anyone's told me since my forever-chasing journey began. And that includes Colby's not-so-real death, which is far-fetched in its own right.

"What can I say?" Pittman asks, shrugging. "The cancer line got me. My dad was in stage four, and so was their friend, and I let him go. Another friend was with him, some guy named Caleb. He's a hacker. He gave me a card and told me they owed me. I never used it because, well, I'm supposed to represent the letter of the law."

So, let's pretend for five minutes that I believe this story. I'll play along and pretend that Pittman was the officer of the day who let these creepy guys go, even with a dead exotic bird in their vehicle. I'll even assume the guy who gave him the card was a legit hacker. But I can't pretend that this won't bite me later.

"Let me get this straight then," Vin says, talking with his hands. "You're going to call in a favor to this Caleb guy and get him to figure out who is blackmailing Drenaline Surf, and you expect me to believe you won't turn us in?"

I can't deny it. Vin and I still think very much alike, very much on the same page. He may not be free-spirited and chasing dreams, but he's rational and realistic. I've missed having another level head around here. Reed and I are often outnumbered.

"I'll make the call," Pittman says. "From my personal phone. You tell me what you need. Fair enough?"

Making deals with the devil isn't something I prefer to do, but Vin is willing to take that risk. He has Pittman make the call, and a guy named Caleb answers. He doesn't reveal his last name, for protection purposes. Smart guy.

After Pittman explains our blackmail situation, Caleb says it won't be a problem.

"Give me about thirty minutes," he says through the phone. "I can hack a bank account pretty easily. Any names in particular I'm looking for?"

We don't give him any. We just ask him to see what he can find. I don't want to tip him off to anyone in particular. We may not be able to use this information legally, but it'll give us an answer – I hope. Then we can work in reverse.

While we wait, Pittman talks about his dad's recent

passing and how blessed he was to be able to spend time with him before it was too late. As an only child with an absent mom and deceased father, I wonder if he sees part of himself in A.J. and that's why he wants to make amends. Maybe he finally gets it or maybe his dad told him to be a man and start doing the right thing. Vin offers condolences just as Pittman's phone rings.

"Hey, you were right about the payoffs," Caleb says through the speaker. "The Burks family is definitely funneling some hardcore cash. They don't even seem to be hiding it. There are about twenty or thirty transfers to this one account."

My heart speeds up, racing like a surfer trying to get through a tube ride before it closes out.

"Can you give us an account number or bank?" Pittman asks.

"I can do better," Caleb says. "I know who's being paid off. You want a name?"

TO BE CONTINUED...

ACKNOWLEDGMENTS

Gabriel. Emily. Jeremy.
Obrigado. Thank you. Merci.

ABOUT THE AUTHOR

Nikki Godwin is a YA contemporary author. Her books are usually about surfers, musicians, or M/M romances. She can't live without Mountain Dew, black eyeliner, and music by Hawthorne Heights. When not writing, she internet-stalks her favorite bands and keeps tabs on surf competitions. Her favorite surfer is Gabriel Medina. If you ever get her started on surfing or music, she'll never shut up. You've been warned.

She also writes stand-alone seaside YA stories under the name Jessa Gabrielle.

DRENALINE SURF SERIES

Chasing Forever Down (Drenaline Surf, #1)
Rough Waters (Drenaline Surf, #2)
Always Summer (Drenaline Surf, #3)
With You Around (Drenaline Surf, #4)

For more information, visit www.nikkigodwin.net

Printed in Poland
by Amazon Fulfillment
Poland Sp. z o.o., Wrocław